BUNGALOW JIM

To my very young granddaughters,
Amelie and Eloise. By the time they reach
adulthood, these tales will be historical fiction.

BUNGALOW JIM

Building tales
from West Wales

Martin Davies

First impression: 2024
© Martin Davies, 2024

Please note: These stories are purely fictional.
Any resemblance to events, people or places,
or names of people or places, is purely coincidental
and nothing should be read into it.

Cover image: Sam Tobias John
Cover design: Martin Davies

ISBN: 978-1-7385604-0-0

Printed in Wales
on paper from well-maintained forests by
Y Lolfa Cyf., Talybont, Ceredigion SY24 5HE
e-mail ylolfa@ylolfa.com
website www.ylolfa.com
tel 01970 832 304

1

SALMON SPREAD

A dark umbrella of cloud has been poised over Tairffynnon, veiling the little town in temporary gloom, but now a breeze picks up, and the shadow moves away to the east, chased at running pace by a tidal wave of sunlit ground which magically transforms everything in its path, washing over the slate roofs of the houses, the awnings of the shops, the messily parked cars and the multi-coloured throng of tourists who spill out into the streets. It floods towards the outskirts of the town, where a new housing estate has sprung up almost overnight, the lush complexion of the green hillside freshly scarred by pot-holed site roads and covered in a rash of bungalows in various stages of completion.

A battered-looking Porsche pulls up on the site. The door flies open, and a squat figure bounds out. Robert James Davies is commonly nicknamed Bungalow Jim, but some dissatisfied customers call him Bungle Jim. He is as wide as he is deep, a sort of cube on legs. But there's no fat to speak of. It's all quite solid. Fronds of black hair shade a pair of canny brown eyes which scan the chaotic site of blockwork, timber and churned-up mud, radiating optimism.

He smiles as he approaches a half-finished bungalow. The boys will be waiting for him like hungry chicks with their beaks open. He leaps through the front door on invisible springs. They come at him from all directions.

'Jim! We need blocks! Now! And sand!'

'They'll be with you today.'

'You said that yesterday.'

'Guaranteed.'

'This bathroom is too small.'

'Put the bath across this wall.'

'In front of the window!'

'They can look out while they're having a bath.'

'This door's going to hit the wall when it opens.'

'Open it outwards.'

When the flood of demands subsides, Jim says: 'Brian and Gary, go and see Mr Bowden, he's complaining about something.'

'We're just finishing the plasterboarding.'

'Forget that, go and see him. Where's Gwyn?'

'He's down a hole.'

Crouched in a manhole, Gwyndaf acknowledges the gift of warm sun on his back with a brief upward glance, then resumes his work. Grunts, complaints and the tic-tic-tic of metal on brick emerge from the hole in the road. Gwyn could be a throwback from a past age; wild and craggy like a piece of Preseli hillside that came loose. The boys call him The Barbarian. He wears wellies and a dirty singlet. His jeans cling desperately to his buttocks, exposing a builder's bum to the passing motorists.

Everything gives way for Gwyn, but this manhole wall won't. He belts it with his hammer and chisel again and again but can't seem to make any impression. Small chips of sharp brick are flying everywhere; up onto the road, down into the sewer, into his eyes, his hair and down his trousers. A shadow falls across his back and he looks up with irritation.

The square, expressive face gazes down, 'Everything alright?'

'Jim, I want a jack-hammer. Now. I can't make a hole through this brick. I've knackered my hand already.' He holds out a bloodied hand in disgust, as if he's disowned it.

Jim's eyes refuse to focus on the mess of blood and ripped skin. 'By-pass the manhole,' he breezes. 'Put a bend in and join into the sewer uphill from it.'

'Don't be dull,' snaps Gwyn. 'You'll never rod it if it blocks.'

'You can rod it from the bungalow. Easy.'

'Those manholes are useless for rodding.'

Jim's no longer listening. He's bounced off. He's forever bouncing; from one place to the next; from one job to the next; from one idea to the next. As problems get thrown at him, he parries and side-steps them like a flyweight boxer. Or if all else fails, he just runs.

Brian is driving the pickup, which bounces along the narrow, high-hedged road to Brynbedw to the accompaniment of crashing and scraping noises as various objects shift about in the back. He is solidly built, close-cropped hair, with a pencil on his ear, denoting that he is a carpenter. His disciple Gary, who sits in the wide passenger seat, is slightly built with a strange mop of bleached hair. As they approach Brynbedw, Gary asks, 'Who is Mr Bowden?'

'Dunno. He came down here from the south-east to retire.'

'Why would people do that? Leave friends and neighbours and family to move to another country?'

'Various reasons. Don't complain. If they didn't, you might

be out of work.' He rounds a bend and is suddenly confronted by an approaching lorry, which fills the road and isn't in a hurry to stop. Brian sweeps into a leafy layby, an old quarry, and pulls up as the lorry thunders past. 'It's our sand.'

'Miracle,' says Gary.

Brian points to the edge of the woods. 'See that gate over there?' It's one of those swing gates that large people have to draw a breath to pass through. It leads down to the river. We're going down there tonight. '

'Fishing?'

'Sort of.'

'Net? Poaching?'

'Maybe. I'm going to London tomorrow, see. I need something to pay for the trip.'

'You take the salmon up with you and sell it up there?'

Brian nods.

Such an important matter, and Brian is telling him, Gary, about it. He decides to push it one stage further. 'Lemme come with you tonight,' he pleads.

Brian snorts in contempt. 'You'll fall in the river.'

'No I won't, honest. Go on.' Then Gary changes tack.' I might tell on you otherwise,' he says half-heartedly. Brian grabs him by the collar and pushes his head back against the seat. 'These boys don't mess about,' he warns as Gary's face changes colour. 'You can come, but don't piss about mind.'

As Brian releases him and sets off again, Gary's face breaks into a badly-suppressed smile.

A vague shape can be seen moving about in the bow window of River View. It comes quite near the glass for a minute, and it's a man's head: round, balding, shiny-red and bespectacled.

Framed in one of the small panes, it looks out on this alien world like a goldfish in a bowl. This is how Mr Bowden feels. He's trapped himself in a small bubble of suburban Slough in a strange land. The bubble extends to the boundaries of his immaculate garden. Beyond is an untamed jungle over which he has no control, where people make empty promises, look blank when he talks to them and infuriate him by speaking in a foreign tongue.

The Bowdens moved to their new bungalow in Brynbedw for economic reasons. Their house in Slough sold for three times the cost of River View, leaving them with a handy nest-egg for their retirement. But west Wales hasn't lived up to Mr Bowden's dreams. He's fallen out of love with the place. The very characteristics he initially found endearing have now become an irritation to him.

It's 3pm. A battered white pickup pulls up, blocking his entrance gates. Scaffolding poles and other building paraphernalia stick out at all angles at the back. Brian and Gary emerge from opposite doors, which slam in unison. Gary mirrors Brian's movements as he lopes reluctantly up the short tarmac drive. 'Whadda we doing here?' he asks the hunched shoulders.

'Dunno, we'll soon find out.' He presses the doorbell, 'Ping-pong.'

'Yappetyyappety yap' goes a dog inside. The door opens. A woolly thing with fangs and beady eyes leaps out at the two figures. It by-passes Brian and heads for Gary, deafening him with its high-pitched barking. Masked from the door by Brian, Gary takes a dummy kick at it, spots Mrs Bowden watching in the bow window and tries unsuccessfully to melt into the concrete paving.

Mr Bowden stands in the doorway, his look of gravity absorbing their tentative smiles of greeting like a sponge. 'So there you are.' His words saw at the air. 'I've only been waiting since nine this morning. Judging by the way you are in these parts, I suppose you could say I'm lucky to see you at all.' They look at the ground and fidget, tired of taking the blame for Jim.

'Why don't you bring them in darling?' chimes a voice from the depths of the hall. They follow Mr Bowden into the house and stomp long-faced into the living room in their boots. He's broken into mime now, glancing back and fore dramatically between them and an invisible spot on the ceiling above the fireplace. Wearily, they wade through the deep-pile carpet, searching the stormy sea of Artex above for the object of his gaze.

Mrs Bowden is a bone china teapot: delicate, refined, and brittle, with a spotless cosy of silver hair. The words pour from her like hot sweet tea. 'We came back from shopping on Friday, we always go shopping on Fridays, don't we dear? It was an awful rainy day and we'd just come in and popped the kettle on. I can't remember why I came into the living room ... that's right, it was to collect the coffee cups ... then I thought, My goodness, I don't remember spilling anything on the floor ...'

Gary and Brian nod repeatedly and shift from one leg to the other like cattle as their eyes glaze over.

'... we didn't notice it at first, you know how it is, anyway, you don't expect a leaky ceiling in a brand new bungalow do you? I called my husband in and he ...'

Brian interrupts: 'I think we'll take a look in the attic. Have you got a torch?'

They greet the attic space with some relief. They pause for a moment to regain their senses. Gary mutters, 'He's a right pain in the arse.'

Brian smiles. 'Wait 'til the floor slab starts to settle. Jim made us throw everything under there.'

They stepping-stone across the ceiling joists to look at the chimney, which glistens with damp in the torchlight. As Brian stretches up to trace the problem, Gary misses his footing and steps on the wet patch of plasterboard.

Downstairs, the Bowdens have been waiting, arms folded, in sceptical silence.

'I do hope they know what they're doing.'

'I doubt it. It's outside they should be looking.'

'They didn't say an awful lot, did they?'

Their words are interrupted by a loud crash as a plimsoled foot bursts unceremoniously into view. It slides down the chimney breast with a terrible squeak and pushes Constable's over-garish canvas-look Haywain off the wall. It hangs there, swinging back and fore, spreading pink and white powder and debris across the living room carpet. Mr and Mrs Bowden stand snap-shot still for a moment, transfixed by this catastrophe in their lives. The dog barks hysterically.

Up in the loft, Brian makes a bolt for the trapdoor. He wants to show himself before Gary has extracted his leg; then it will be obvious, without telling on Gary, who the guilty party was. He reaches the living room door just in time to witness the offending limb return to its attic domain like a clip from a science fiction B-movie.

As Gary reaches the ladder, he decides to deflect some anger by feigning injury. 'Oh! Oh! Oh!' he groans and staggers down the rungs, missing the last few steps altogether for extra effect.

Mrs Bowden's anger turns to instant sympathy. She rushes forward to mother him. 'You poor thing, are you badly hurt? Darling, he's hurt himself.'

Mr Bowden has crossed the anger barrier into numbness, shock and disbelief. As Gary has now been engulfed in a cocoon of sympathy, he turns on Brian. 'I want this mended today,' he wheezes, 'not tomorrow, d'you hear me?'

'Yes Mr Bowden, but we'll have to get plasterboard. We'll be back in half an hour.'

'I've heard that before.'

'No, definite, guaranteed.'

Back in the pickup, Brian says 'I'm not going back there again, that's for sure.'

'Nor me neither, no way,' says Gary.

After Brian and Gary depart from Brynbedw, the day wears on and the sun gives out less and less heat until it finally sinks with a shiver behind the bungalows. The air itches with a million gnats, chased by the dark shapes of bats that twist this way and that, uttering tiny pinching sounds. Someone is cooking supper. The smell wafts over on the breeze.

As it gets dark, the moon rises over the hill, straw-coloured and huge. You could reach out and touch it. The hours pass. The bungalows go to sleep one by one. By midnight, all is as quiet as a picture. But wait. What's this? Four dark figures, or is it five? In the layby. Swift and silent, they steal through the swing gate and melt into the woodland. Their stroboscopic outlines dart among the trees in the dappled moonlight as they descend to the river. That swing gate was the portal to a bygone age. They've become ancient Celtic hunters now, lost in a time warp. Their prey is hardly dramatic and the danger not exactly mortal; but it's enough and imagination can supply the rest. Their excitement is tangible, heightened by the chill in the air and the many mysterious sounds which emerge from the tangled blackness.

They quickly reach the river and instinctively crouch low in the comparative exposure of the riverbank. A tall figure, stern and serious, motions them to follow. Could this be the same Elfed Rees who works at the Co-op? What happened to that subservient figure, bent over a till that goes 'beep bop, beep bop' all day? In his fishy mischief on that timeless dusky riverbank, an Elfed Rees of new-found stature and dignity leads his gang through the long grass.

It's 5.30am. Mr Bowden dreams that the whole ceiling has caved in under a deluge of water. He sees that youth with the bleached hair perched on the joists looking down at him with a triumphant grin. Tricksy is barking up at him. On and on. He doesn't stop.

Mr Bowden awakes. But the barking goes on. Grumpily, he struggles down to the hall, where Tricksy jiggles about, wagging his tail, pawing at the front door. He obviously wants to do his business. He opens the door and the dog bolts out.

He's awake now, so Mr Bowden dresses and goes outside. Tricksy has vanished. There's only the empty road, the humming of milking machines on the nearby farm and the dawn chorus. He heads for a path which leads down through the woods to the river. Tricksy will have gone this way out of habit. It's a beautiful sunrise, not a soul in sight. Mr Bowden feels like lord of the manor. He leaves the dazzle of the meadow and ventures into the trees. There's a little swing gate to negotiate. Tricksy will have squeezed through a gap in the fence as he always does.

When he emerges at the water's edge, the air is quite cold and clammy, eerily still. A creamy mist over the surface of the water is gradually lifting and the dark green reflection of the trees on the opposite bank materialises in its place. A rustling in the undergrowth makes him jump. It's Tricksy; a few pounds of orange fluff heading towards him through the long grass. He whines to be picked up and in his master's arms he judders nervously.

'What's the matter, old son?' asks Mr Bowden. At the same time, upstream, he notices what appear to be pieces of bread floating on the water. But they don't follow the current, and they are all in a straight line, like white stepping stones, reaching a good halfway across the river. He goes nearer to investigate. The 'pieces of bread' are floats, supporting an invisible net below. He goes to where the net has been pegged to the bank, puts Tricksy down and begins to draw it up. It's green, gut-like, and hard to hold. As he lifts it, at first there are only leaves and a few rotted sticks, but raising it just that little bit further reveals the first small sewin struggling limply in its mesh. The gut has torn through the scales and dark blood oozes down the body as it hangs, helpless, just clear of the water.

Only then does it occur him that the net must have an owner. Or owners. They must be near. Poachers. Tricksy has gone quiet, hugging the ground. Mr Bowden gets an odd feeling, something he has already half-registered. He looks to his left and there, not fifteen yards away, sees four men sat on the slope in a row, half under the trees. Betrayed by the lifting mist, they look straight ahead, silent, Sphinx-like. They could be ghosts, the way they don't appear to see him. They have seen him of course. Taken by surprise, they have been sitting stock-still and watching him all along; watched him part-pull up their net, and now they are still watching without looking. Three of them are complete strangers, but the fourth ... even in the dim light, there's no mistaking the fourth.

By 8.30am, the day has lost its promise. Someone up there pressed the wrong button. Suddenly, there's wind and rain. It isn't normal vertical rain. It's the Welsh type: horizontal rain. For a moment, Tairffynnon is almost blotted out and the blurred forms of Jim's new bungalows are just visible against a charcoal grey sky. Everywhere, bleak figures race for cover. But not Gwyn. He carries on exactly as before. To him, the slightest concession to the rain would mean surrender. Even when drips fall from his carrot-red hair into his cauliflower ear, he doesn't brush them off, or the rain will have won. He squats at the base of the deep trench, fitting together the last pieces of drain, slithering about like a mud-wrestler. Occasionally, he bellows orders to his hooded helper, who splashes back and fore, fetching things. John is a lean, good-natured Englishman with an ingratiating smile; prematurely grey and a little frail looking. The orders are in Welsh, but the technical words are often in English, so that he usually understands.

'*Dere* file *i fi.*'

'*Cer i mofyn* slip coupling, *wnei di.*'

But secretly, the rain is getting to Gwyn. He begins to punish the drain parts as he fits them together. Teeth gritted, he saws them apart as they wail for mercy. He files the ends until they scream. He twists them into the collars, finalising the torture with a numbing blow from a lump hammer at the opposite end. He doesn't notice the two figures leaping into the trench until a dirty-looking carrier bag is held under his nose and he smells fish.

'Look what we've got, Gwyn.'

'Uh?'

'Salmon. Not bad eh?'

'Nnn.'

Brian and Gary look tired but triumphant. But then their expressions change. Something has pulled up on site. They drop the fish and peep over the trench wall, their chins almost touching the ground. They blink as raindrops bounce into their eyes. From this rodent's viewpoint, they see two vehicles: a white van and a familiar looking car. Out of the car steps Mr Bowden. They both crouch down in the trench.

'Hide the fish! Hide the fish!' whispers Brian. He passes it to Gary, who passes it back as if it's a bomb about to go off.

'Give it 'ere!' commands Gwyn wearily, ripping the greasy carrier bag from Brian's grasp. Then without changing his pace, he calmly offsets the open drain ends, slips the package in one end, brings them back in line and begins tapping the slip coupling in place. Exit one salmon.

But Gary knows he's going to be identified. He's having one of his panics. He squats in the trench with his hands on his head, wiggling his knees.

'*Iesu Grist*, calm down will you!' Brian says in disgust.

'It's alright for you, innit? He didn't see you.'

'I had the sense to hide, that's why.'

They hear voices approaching. Two figures appear, towering over them at the edge of the trench. One is of course Mr Bowden, the other the water bailiff. The water bailiff is stockily built and wears a dark green, hooded waterproof jacket, trousers and olive green wellies. His face, what's visible of it, has a kindly expression. Too soft you might think for a water bailiff. But take another look. The eyes have a subtle hardness and the jaw more than a hint of firmness. This man can look after himself alright.

There's a moment of silence while everyone stands there dripping, wondering what's going to happen next. Then Mr Bowden points an accusing finger at Gary. 'That's the one,' he barks with a self-satisfied look. Gary cowers visibly. Brian looks away with an ill-concealed grin.

'Might I have a word with you, young man?' asks the bailiff, then reaching for Gary's hand, he hauls him out of the trench. The questioning begins in subdued tones, but soon Gary's protesting voice is loud enough for the others to hear.

'I haven't done nothing! He 's only saying that because I made a hole in his ceiling.'

'Absolute poppycock!' retorts Mr Bowden.

The bailiff turns to Mr Bowden. 'What led you to believe that this young man was present?'

'It was obvious.'

'Even in poor light?'

'Even in poor light.'

'Was his face turned towards you?'

'Well no, but you can spot that hair anywhere,' says Mr Bowden, defensive, with disgruntlement beginning to set in.

'Other people have a hairstyle like this,' pipes up Gary.

'Who in particular?' asks the bailiff.

'If I told you, you'd be picking on them next.'

During the questioning, Jim appears on site and it magically stops raining. Keeping a discreet distance from the confrontation, he bounds across to survey the completed drain. What should have been a straight line to the manhole has now taken an awkward deviation ending in a saddle onto the main sewer. It's cost more than getting Gwyn a jack-hammer and taken more time. Another one of Jim's long shortcuts. He frowns. He doesn't like that bend. Better get it covered before the building inspector sees it.

'Ok, get it filled over,' he shouts down. They look hesitant. The salmon is still in there and the enemy is still watching.

'Come on. Don't just stand there. I want this JCB in Felinwen in half an hour.'

'We haven't got any pea gravel.'

'Come on, don't fuss. Anything will do. Just fill it in. Now.'

Typical isn't it? For once, Jim doesn't just bounce off. He's adopted a rare statuesque pose. He doesn't budge.

Gwyn gets out of the trench and jumps resignedly into the digger. It leaps into action. A primate in charge of a dinosaur. The arm swings around dangerously. Most of the excavated material has gone elsewhere, so backfilling becomes a site clearing exercise. Everything goes into this trench. The bucket makes a dismissive gesture and hunks of broken block hurtle down. You can hear plasticky thuds as the thinly-covered drain tries not to break. Through the long grass, other items come to light: a pile of rotting cement bags, abstract sculptures of discarded mortar and plaster, a palette, the rusting base of a wheelbarrow. With a callous sideways sweep and merciless ripping sounds, the metal arm tears indiscriminately through the lot and shoves it over the side.

It's Friday night now as the pickup splashes its way along the road to Brynbedw. Inside, Gary, Sue and Brian sit in a row along the seat. Brian is driving. Gary can't believe the transformation in the pickup. It's going to London, that's why. Only this morning, the back was full of scaffolding and odds and ends and the cab was a dusty mess of tools, drain parts, lunchboxes and foot-printed delivery notes. Now, the back is empty apart from drain rods and an ice box. The cab is spotless. Before, it smelt of soil, cement, farts and sweaty bodies. Now there's an all-pervading aroma. The air is filled with the Sueness of Sue.

Brian's girlfriend wears black velvet trousers and a black silky blouse. Gary's right-hand side is in contact with her from her ankles all the way up to her shoulders. Her mood changes pass through to him like electric currents. He hopes she doesn't spot the two-inch gap between his left-hand side and the passenger door. Occasionally, she shakes her head from side to side and a mop of long, curly black hair caresses his face. He almost forgets his predicament until Brian reminds him.

'Cheer up Gary, there must be worse places than Swansea nick.'

Sue elbows him, but Brian ignores her. With one hand on the wheel, he nonchalantly hauls the pickup round a sharp bend, then returns to his prey.

'Some people enjoy it there, don't want to come home. Mind you, Dai Penllyn had a bad time when he first went.' He pauses, waiting for Gary to prompt him. The wipers count time: 'wump wump, wump wump.'

'What happened?' asks Gary hesitantly, not wanting to know.

'They tied his balls to the bed frame and he was stuck like that all night. Didn't dare move see. 'Brian glances across to see Gary's reaction. Trying not to grin, Sue smacks Brian over the head. The pickup veers momentarily off course.

Gary brings his knees together instinctively. 'Was he alright?'

'No problem. He had two children already. He didn't want any more anyway.'

Gary looks preoccupied. He stares fixedly ahead.

'Don't listen to him', says Sue, gazing at him protectively, 'you won't be going to prison.' She flashes him a gorgeous smile and he basks in her sunshine. For the moment, enveloped in her aura, he feels oblivious to anything.

It's a black, wet night as they pull onto Jim's site. You can just see the lights of the village, bleary-eyed, through the trees. A car swishes by on the road. They slip silently out of the cab and Brian reaches for the drain rods out of the back.

Sue shines the torch into Brian's face. 'Gerraway!' He swats at the beam with his hand. Sue erupts into giggles, tickled by the stupidity of the situation and the seriousness of his expression. She head-butts him in the chest; he shrugs her off. She trips on something and careers into the pickup. More giggles. Gary laughs with her until Brian freezes them.

'Stop it will you!' he barks. 'We've got to go to London tonight.' He wanders off. You can hear a door being opened and footsteps thumping on a hut floor. The torch picks him out as he emerges with two manhole keys. The boys wander down to the main road. Sue scuttles behind, shivering a little and trying to stay serious.

There's no traffic, so they lift up the manhole cover. Sue reaches over, birdlike, and shines the torch into the depths.

'*Ych*, that's bloody disgusting.'

'Go on then, jump in.' Brian hands Gary the torch and practically pushes him in. As he lands at the bottom, his feet spread out and he straddles the open drain.

'You're very brave,' says Sue.

Gary glows. 'Who's going to direct the traffic?' he asks, trying to sound casual and cheerful.

'No need,' comes the gruff reply.

'The cars might fall in the hole.'

'There's a cast iron reason why they won't, 'says Brian, then drops the lid with a heavy 'clung' back into the frame.

Suddenly and unexpectedly entombed, Gary becomes instantly claustrophobic and he remembers stories about alligators breeding in the sewers. Fighting back a panic wave, he shines the torch upwards, just as a metallic voice booms down from a keyhole in the lid. It fades. There's the roar of an approaching vehicle which becomes almost deafening. Strands of light whip round the dank walls, then the roaring recedes. Water drips onto his head. The dismembered voice returns. He half hears.

'I'm going to rod the … grab salmon as it comes through … miss it you can bl… stay down there.'

Gary shines the torch down at the awful river that passes under his feet. The stench possesses him. He waits and waits, all the time poised to grab the salmon as it comes past.

An aeon passes. No salmon. Has he failed to spot it? The torch begins to dim. He wants to cry out, but he knows they won't hear. He reaches up to lift the lid, but he's in an awkward position. It won't budge. Maybe they've gone to London and left him … after all, this was his fault. Was this all a ploy to punish him? Invisible hands of despair clutch at him; they squeeze his stomach into a knot.

What if they have a car accident and get killed on the M4? Nobody will ever know where he is. It could be weeks, months maybe, before his body is found, probably eaten by rats. He supposes someone will smell him, but you expect bad smells to come from a sewer. It could be years. He can see his mother now, tearfully appearing on the TV, appealing for help.

'Have you any idea where he might be?' asks the reporter, his face a picture of concern.

No, replies his mother, her voice shaking with emotion, 'I know he was in some kind of trouble, I hope … I hope he hasn't … done anything stupid. He's a good boy really you know.

'ARE YOU THERE STILL?'

Gary jumps. He nearly drops the torch.

'Yes.'

'Well answer me. Help me get the lid up. It's jammed tight.'

The air above ground is like wine. It's good to be alive.

'What happened?' asks Gary, climbing to his feet. 'I didn't see no fish, honest.'

'Those manholes are rubbish. You can't rod the drains. That's the end of my salmon. Shit!' He's in a black mood. He kicks at the air as they walk back to the pickup.

Sue gazes at Gary with concern. 'Are you alright? It must have been horrible down there.'

'Come on, forget him. Let's go!' Brian shoves her in and shuts the pickup door.

'What about Gary?'

'He can walk home.' The pickup burns off up the road and a dark, gloomy figure, head bent, can't be seen walking back towards town.

It's the following morning. Gary's sat at the kitchen table, looking glum. He battles through a slice of toast and sips thoughtfully at his tea. His mum is stood nearby at the kitchen unit. The debris of sandwich-making is spread all around her. She's only about five feet two, petite, with brown hair she still keeps long. She wears a rugby shirt, tight-fitting jeans she's forced herself into and a permanent look of dogged perseverance. She pushes the last sandwich down into the lunch box. It springs back a little. Then in a gap, she adds a hard-boiled egg, an apple and a Penguin bar. She says, 'That Brian is a bad influence on you.'

'Oh Mum, I'm grown up now, I'm twenty-one.'

'Still young enough to be led astray.' She shuts the sandwich box lid with finality and glances up to check the clock.

'Brrrrrring!' the doorbell rings and they both jump. Gary's mum disappears down the corridor. She re-emerges followed by the water bailiff, who ducks as he comes through the kitchen door. A large butterfly settles in Gary's stomach.

Gary's mum pulls out a chair. 'Can I make you some tea?' The kettle whistles as if to confirm the offer.

'No thank you Sheila, I won't stay long.' The water bailiff perches on the edge of the chair and looks at Gary. 'Young man, I've decided not to pursue this any further, because it's a matter of identification and you weren't caught red-handed.' The butterfly in Gary's stomach gets ready for take-off. He fights with his face muscles to suppress a grin.

'But if your name pops up again in connection with poaching, I might not be so lenient next time. I would advise you in future to be more careful about the company you keep.'

Sheila, standing hidden behind the bailiff, nods emphatically in agreement.

Wet and windy summer gradually changes to wet and windy autumn. More by default than planning, the new bungalows at Tairffynnon gradually near completion. They don't actually reach completion. No bungalow of Jim's actually reaches completion. As Jim says, 'If you don't leave them something to moan about, they won't be happy, will they? If you spoil them and finish everything, they'll only find faults that aren't there.'

One by one, the bungalows are occupied; lawns are seeded, tidy cars sit in their garages and the new residents moan to each other regularly over their fences about Jim.

'I phoned him up three times yesterday and he promised he would be here this morning.'

'Promises, promises, it's all a load of hot air.'

'And you should see the boot marks those men left on my carpet.'

'Not so much as a by your leave.'

'Nobody gives a damn these days.'

'Exactly.'

Among Jim's boys, the lost salmon has become a legend. Like a fallen hero, it grows daily in stature. They eulogise it in glowing terms. But deep down in its orange plastic coffin, the fabled fish, slowly decomposing in its carrier bag, doesn't get to rest in peace. For a while, it resists the bombardment from flushing toilets, washing machines and baths, but a build-up of pressure finally sets it on the move.

Once in motion, the unsavoury package successfully negotiates the bend and heads at speed towards the junction with the sewer. Entering the main flow breaks its back. The carrier bag begins to open out. It manages to enter the road manhole, but blocks the far end. The level in the manhole begins to rise.

Jim is showing Mr and Mrs Endsleigh around their bungalow-to-be on plot 4. It's one of his 'Poplars' designs, but it's been pruned and altered so much, it bears little resemblance to the original.

Mr Endsleigh wears a blue corduroy cap (he fancies himself as a bit of a sailor). His bushy grey beard is immaculately trimmed round the edges, as his lawn will soon be. His jeans and woolly jumper just don't seem right on him somehow.

Mrs Endsleigh ('Please call me Pauline') has mid-length straight dyed hair. It flaps like a spaniel's ears as she moves her head. She wears her jumper and slacks with a certain severity.

Jim is standing at the bathroom door now. He invites them in with a flourish. Pauline looks round the door and her face freeze-dries. Jim looks for the dead body that must be lying in the bath.

'But I wanted the Whisper Peach bathroom suite, not the Whisper Grey,' she whines with despair.

'I bet you did,' thinks Jim, 'but there was a 30 per cent discount on this one.' He adopts a look of charming sincerity. 'We'll have it changed, no problem, it's nothing.'

Pauline relaxes for a second, then homes in on him again. 'But what about the matching tiles?'

'No problem.'

Pauline looks completely satisfied. As soon as they leave, she expects workmen in (matching) overalls to magically transform this bathroom to Whisper Peach in a matter of hours. How can she know that this will happen on exactly the same day as a large herd of pigs flies over Tairffynnon?

We're standing in the living room now, admiring the 'feature fireplace', a bizarre sculpture of bricks and crazy paving. The Endsleighs are impressed and Jim is happy too because he used up a lot of leftovers here. And they won't find out that the flue draws badly until they try to burn the Yule log at Christmas and set off the smoke alarm.

Something catches Jim's eye. He glances out of the window and blanches. Damn! It's none other than Mr Bowden walking up the drive towards them. And he's looking confrontational. Jim frowns. The Endsleighs haven't signed on the dotted line yet. He can't afford to let old man Bowden poison them. How is he going to defuse him? Head for the danger. That's the answer. He edges the Endsleighs towards the front door.

Mr Bowden is about to deliver three hard knocks when the front door flies open and catches him off his guard.

'Edward!' exclaims Jim, smiling down at him. 'Meet Mr and Mrs Endsleigh. They only live down the road from your home town.'

'Oh,' says Mr Bowden, suppressing a scowl. 'And where's that?'

'Maidstone.'

'I come from Slough. That must be at least sixty miles away. Hardly down the road.' The Endsleighs laugh at Jim's expense. A shoulder laugh. Jim is happy right now to be the butt of any amusement. He holds a good-natured grin in place with invisible tape. 'This is Phil and this is Pauline. Edward Bowden.'

'I was stationed at Maidstone,' announces Mr Bowden, stiffening into a military stance.

'How interesting.' Pauline beams at him. He flushes. The pink goes all the way up between the thinning hairs on his scalp. He imagines her in a freshly-pressed army uniform. He quivers. A nostalgic whiff of canvas and dubbin invades his nostrils. He mentally smacks her khaki-skirted bottom, bold as brass, as she scours out a mess-tin.

It only took minutes for the manhole to fill, then little jets of foul liquid spurted through the keyholes of the lid. The pressure increases now as the sewage backs up the pipe.

'Pwang!' the cover has blown. It sidesteps about a foot. An unspeakable pond quickly begins to fill a dip in the road where Mr Bowden has left his car. The unfinished drive of the Endsleighs' bungalow was too messy for it. A vanguard wave of raw sewage approaches it now with silent stealth. Lapping gently, it nuzzles the rear tyres, engulfing them in its sickly embrace, before creeping hungrily towards the front pair. Slowly but surely it rises, licking the shining hub-caps, eagerly nibbling at the freshly-polished paintwork.

2
TIGER

The Bowdens' bungalow is suffering a temporary return to the wild. Hammering, boisterous conversation and raucous laughter waft through their precious sanctuary on treacly waves of beer vapour, violating rooms that have been so painstakingly tamed.

Gwyn is out mending the leaking chimney, but Brian, Gary and John have opted for a more leisurely Friday afternoon. Fixing the damaged living-room ceiling presents a vague focus of minimal energy shared amongst three, a social gathering with a hint of work. The Bowdens are in Swansea. They didn't dare put Jim off, so they gave him the key with a lot of express provisos, but only the key got passed onto Brian.

The hole in the ceiling has lain dormant for weeks, providing a melodramatic conversation-piece for unsuspecting guests. Now it's been enlarged, squared off and filled with a new piece of plasterboard. Some of the plaster dropped onto the newspaper they put here and there on the floor, but most is being ground into the carpet by several pairs of boots.

Only the Artex remains to do, so it's time for a wander and to poke into things. Brian begins to extract the Bowdens' classical record collection from a veneered cabinet behind the TV. What's this? 'Moat's Fart'. He slings it onto the bookshelf.

'Here's a good one: Viv the Baldy.' He picks up another. 'Hey this name is weird, mun. The writing's got bits above it.' He holds it under Gary's nose. 'Whassis say?'

Gary smiles wanly. 'I dunno.'

'John, come 'ere boy, whassis say?'

'I think it's pronounced Dvor-jac.'

'Dv-or-jac.' Open the Dvor, Jac. Ha ha! Who'sis? List.'

'I bet he was pissed,' offers Gary.

'Shaddup,' Brian pauses, flicking through more sleeves. 'Hey, there's a Welsh one here: Bach. *Bach* means small in Welsh, see John.'

'I know.'

'Called him that because he had a little one, see.' He looks at Gary with that broad, confident grin of his which demands appreciation. Gary grins with him, then picks up the remote control, aims at the telly and presses the buttons aimlessly. A disjointed cacophony of unfinished sentences assaults the air as he runs through the channels.

Just inside the kitchen door, Tricksy has been maintaining an uneasy silence. No barking or heroics today. Curled up in his basket for security, he's been keeping a low profile. But when he looks up to see Brian's intimidating stare, you can hear snuffling noises as he licks himself nervously and constantly shifts about in his basket.

'He looks like Chops' dog,' observes Brian, leaning casually against the door frame as if he owns the place.

'Maybe,' says Gary, casting a brief glance around the door, 'same model I suppose.' He hates this dog.

'Dogs don't have models you fool, it's not a car.'

'I dunno, same make whatever. The hair's the same colour too.' He points the remote control at it, pretends to zap it, wishing it dead. 'Die dog!' Tricksy cringes in his basket.

John is absent-mindedly inspecting the china animals on the mantelpiece. Brian brushes him aside and clumsily begins to re-arrange them with ominous clinking noises. He stands back with a dramatic sweep of the arm to reveal six animals mounting each-other in a row. 'Daraaa! Might as well be happy if they're stuck here all day,' he reasons.

'Who's this then?' asks Gary, pointing at Mr Bowden's army photo on the TV.

'The man himself,' says Brian, picking up a magazine.

'Bowden? It doesn't look much like him.'

'That's because he's younger, you idiot. This is crap.' He lobs the magazine onto the floor with disdain.

Gary picks up a stapler, opens it out, and starts firing staples at the photo with a manic stare. 'Cla-clic! Cla-clic!' A pile of spent staples gathers on top of the TV and on the floor. Brian rips it from his grasp and smacks him over the head.

'Well, well, what have we here?'

Two heads whirl round in unison. John has opened a cupboard and an array of bottles gleams from the dark interior.

'Drinks all round!' shouts Brian. He bounds across the room, plunges his hand in and takes out a large bottle of Scotch. The other two look hesitant. He starts picking the crystal glasses from the shelf.

'Get The Barbarian.'

Gwyn is out on the roof, scaling the roof-ladder, panther-like, with a piece of lead in one hand and tin-snips in his teeth. He ignores Gary until he reaches the chimney. Then he fits the lead between the rungs, spits the tin-snips into his cupped hands, turns down to Gary and snarls, 'Whaddoo you want?'

Then with that same light, catlike movement, he descends the ladder.

Once in the house, he glances in momentarily at the assembled company before wandering down the passage to the bathroom. The sound of copious urination reverberates through the house.

Generous helpings of Scotch are being passed around. Gwyn returns from the bathroom, doing up his flies. He accepts the drink out of good manners; he would prefer to be out on the roof.

Through the bow window, the afternoon sky has gone to look cold and bleak. A strong wind is shaking the scraggy trees on the top field to and fro. Bluey-grey clouds slip across the horizon as if in a hurry to get home. The Scotch tastes good.

Gary's gone quiet. He's been flicking through some photos he found on their side in the drinks cupboard. They're holiday snaps. He stops on one, and his face comes over all soppy. As he lingers on it, the boys crowd round. She's a girl of about twenty-one, slim but solid, wearing a red and white striped swimsuit. Still wet from the sea, she sits in the sand facing the camera, balancing a Coke bottle on her up-raised knees. A shock of yellow tousled hair cascades in orderly disorder over her reddy-brown shoulders. There's just the trace of a squint in those bright blue eyes, giving her an air of mischief. The flared nostrils make her look self-assured and her lips are full and generous.

Gary doesn't hear the murmurs of approval or notice that the others are looking over his shoulder. He's completely engrossed, rescuing her from certain death by drowning and carrying her limp body back onto the beach. Sweeping everyone aside, he skilfully administers the kiss of life. Her eyes open languidly and, eternally grateful and smitten by his dashing looks, she clasps him to her firm bosom with her lanky arms. She's his for life.

'*Iesu Grist*, that must be the Bowdens' daughter,' says Brian, snatching the photo from Gary, who starts, rudely awakened from his reverie.

'Hey gerroff, that's mine ...'

But Brian has already fallen under her spell. They meet at a late-night disco in Portugal and at two in the morning, he leads her by the hand down onto the moonlit beach. Without a word, they strip naked and walk hand in hand into the dark waters, where they make passionate love in the shallows. She moans 'Oh Brian!' a number of times. After frolicking about in the waves, they retire to the sand-dunes where she surrenders once more to his irresistible charms.

'She's a good-looker alright,' says John.

Gwyn grunts. A deep, animal grunt, straight from the gut.

'It think it likes her,' says Brian.

A spell has been cast over Jim's boys. That single shiny snap has brought on a religious revival. A distinctly uncharacteristic aura of respect has possessed them. Right away, Gary has collected all the glasses and taken them into the kitchen to wash them. John is mixing up Artex and he's laid out a large sheet he found in the pickup under the repaired ceiling. After re-arranging the animals on the mantelpiece, Brian has found another whisky bottle and poured a little into the one that's drastically reduced in level. Now he takes both to the kitchen sink, shoves Gary out of the way and tops them up with water to a respectable height. You almost have to wade through the goodness and morality that hangs in the air.

And that's not all. Odd crashing and clanking noises emanate from a cupboard in the hall. Gwyn emerges noisily, wrestling with a vacuum cleaner, tube and cable flying everywhere, a look of intense concentration on his face. In goes the plug with a thump and it bursts into life, allowing him to comb every fibre of the carpet with the tube, like a monkey searching in its fur for fleas.

The front door suddenly bursts open. In strides Jim, ready to move mountains. 'How's it going, boys? It's getting cold outside.' As he rubs his hands together, the door catches in the wind and crashes against the wall. If you released a spring, it wouldn't move as fast as Tricksy does when he feels the draught from that door. He crosses the living room like a guided canine missile, clatters across the hall, taking the corner on two paws, and bolts outside. All Jim sees is a honey-coloured blur.

'Make sure you don't let the dog out,' he remembers Mr Bowden repeating in his ear.

'Oh dear!'

Tricksy shoots down the garden path and bounds through the gate at the end, his spiky fur hardly touching the bars as he catapults himself onto the road. A flash of red whizzes past and there's a frantic screech of tyres followed by a loud thump like someone smacking a cushion hard. The boys freeze in action like waxworks until a groan from Jim makes them head for the door and run out onto the road.

Tricksy is lying by the verge, twitching, wriggling and whimpering pathetically. There's a large, odd-shaped hole in the side of his belly with blood oozing out of it. His fur is all matted with oily dirt and one of his eyes has been knocked clean out, a shiny red orb, hanging peculiarly from the socket. There's no car in sight.

Nobody knows what to do.

'Perhaps we should put him out of his misery,' suggests John.

'Yeah, better hit him on the head with a piece of three by two,' says Brian unsentimentally, 'I'll get some from the pickup.

'No, we'll have to call a vet,' says Jim with a look of despair.

Just then, Tricksy breathes his last doggy breath and dies.

Five men stand round a dead dog on a windswept lane at 3.30pm, saying nothing.

Gary is a little perturbed as he looks down at the grubby piece of snuffed-out fluff on the tarmac. Not half an hour ago, he wished this dog dead and now here it is, lifeless at his feet. Maybe he possesses psychic powers and has brought this about. This dog could be … hardly living proof… more like very dead proof of some hitherto undiscovered gift. He remembers having bad thoughts about Mrs Jenkins the dinner lady at school and she was gone just days later. A stroke or something. A stroke of luck he thought at the time, but he felt curiously guilty when he learnt of her demise.

Suddenly he thinks of Mr Bowden. He was flicking staples at his photograph. Maybe he'll get pumped full of bullets in a bank raid in Swansea …

'Gaaaaary!'

'Yes, Jim.'

'Let's get this dog onto the property out of sight.' Jim glances over the road to make sure nobody's witnessed the tragedy. Gary and John dither around the body, wondering where to get hold of it. Gwyn pushes them aside, grabs it by the scruff of the neck, walks through the gate with it, then throws it on the lawn, where it goes into a kind of banana shape. They re-group around the corpse while Jim puzzles over what to do next.

Jim had been hoping to squeeze the £5,000 he is still owed out of Mr Bowden, but when the latter finds out what has happened to his dog, it seems out of the question for even Jim to pull this one off.

'What are we going to do?' asks Jim. 'They're due home before dark.'

'Tell them their bloody hound is dead,' says Gwyn.

'I can't, they'll go apeshit,' pleads Jim, concealing the real reason.

'So, tough,' says Gwyn, with a bovine look. He's already losing interest.

'Maybe you could swop it with Chops' dog,' suggests Brian nonchalantly.

'Chops has got a dog like this?' Jim's head suddenly bristles with antennae.

Brian adopts that cool, informative look. 'Same make, same model, same year probably,' he says, borrowing Gary's earlier description. Jim has gone pensive. He scratches his wiry locks briskly. Ideas are brewing in there.

'You're not seriously thinking of swopping dogs?' asks Brian, with a worried frown.

'Anyway, it wouldn't work,' says Gary. 'Chops' dog is Welsh.

'Oh yeah,' Brian retorts, 'it talks Welsh does it? You pillock.'

'No, but if it doesn't lie down and things, when it's told to, Bowden's going to wonder.'

'He's right,' says Jim, 'but we don't need him for very long.

All he has to do is run out of the house when Bowden opens the door and disappear into this hedge here.' He points to the hedge between the Bowdens and the next-door field.

'But he went out through the gate,' says John.

'Nobody knows that. We can plant the body anywhere up the road.'

'What about the squeal of tyres, you've got to have that,' insists Gary, the excitement raising his voice an octave.

'Maybe if you must,' Jim reluctantly concedes. 'Right.' He's ready to bounce. 'John, I want you to finish in the house. Gwyn ...'

But Gwyn has already left the gathering in disgust. Gary watches as he climbs up the roof, his bulky form casting a sinister silhouette against the winter sky. He could be one of those mystery wild animals people report that they have seen, thinks Gary. A puma or something. The Beast of Brynbedw! He imagines Mrs Bowden coming out of the house after her television viewing has been disturbed by odd noises on the roof. She looks up just as the thing leaps down at her. She screams: 'Waaaaaaaaaaaaaaaaaaaaaah!' then runs hell for leather down the road with padding footsteps behind her getting nearer and nearer.

'Gary!'

'Nn?'

'You two had better come with me in the pickup. Hide the dog behind that bush.'

Tairffynnon is busy this afternoon and in a state of glorious chaos. The double-yellow lines on both sides of the road are almost blotted out by parked cars and the through-traffic is constantly being held up by buses and lorries inching their way through gaps or sounding their horns for car owners to emerge from shops to shift their vehicles. People cross the road in front of the vehicles with apparent disregard for life and limb. Some very shaky hymn-singing is drifting out of The Plough interspersed with juke-box music. 'Breeeeeeaaad of Heeeeaaaaven, Breeeeeeaaad of Heeeeaaaven, thump, thump thump.'

Jim pulls up outside the butcher's shop and heaves the right-hand wheels over the kerb and onto the pavement. He turns to the boys, says, 'Right, I'll be ten minutes,' then bolts like a rabbit through the door of the shop. Brian and Gary turn to each-other with blank expressions.

'Let's go and have a pint,' suggests Brian. 'Your round.'

The pickup doors slam as the two figures slope off down the High Street, Brian swaggering and looking round for talent, Gary doing his best to copy him.

Chops' butcher's shop used to be full of character: mahogany counters and slabs of marble, well-worn wooden floorboards sprinkled with sawdust and protruding nails polished by all the foot traffic, faded posters of various meats peeling off the walls, change coming back into your hand as blood-and-gut covered notes. But the Environmental Health have been and given the place the kiss of death. The walls, which were plastered and painted, are now covered in laminate; the floors are plastic-tiled, new streamlined counters have been fitted, everything is served in squeaky polythene. But worst insult of all, the boys have to wear silly hats on their heads.

But as for Chops, all that paraphernalia is a thin veneer. He still has the same boar-like face, with the large, curly eyebrows, the stomping walk and of course that vicious, bone-splintering chop. He doesn't like Jim; as soon as he spots him, he starts chopping harder. 'Clunk, clunk, clunk.' The whole shop shakes with the blows he is raining down on this piece of meat. Jim three-quarters built a bungalow for his brother. There aren't going to be any favours here. Money will have to change hands.

Something else hasn't changed: the scrum. Like all local shops, there's no queue; instead, there's a melee. But all very well-mannered; amazingly, everyone seems to know who's next. Anyone who steps out of line is likely to get 'told straight', however. This is what happens to Jim now, as he walks past everyone and goes up to Chops.

'Well,' puffs a dumpy little lady next-but-one to Jim, 'don't bother to wait your turn, will you.' She peeks round her scarf at the others, hoping for moral support. Jim offers her a pleasant smile, but doesn't bother to explain himself.

'*Ga' i air 'da chi?*' He wants a word.

Chops leads Jim through a laminate-faced door that is almost part of the wall. They step back in time to a tiny room which is dominated by a threadbare three-piece suite and a rickety table. Mugs and biscuits are laid out on the table, together with an old silvery kettle with a frayed lead. The air is full of dust from the upholstery.

'Yappetyyappety yap,' comes from the room beyond.

'Better tell me what you want then, you're in that much of a hurry,' says Chops with a frown. 'If you want to build something for me, the answer is no.' He plonks himself down on the settee, wearing a distinctly uncooperative look. The dust level in the air increases dramatically.

'That's what it is, I want to borrow your dog,' says Jim with a charming smile, as if he was asking the time.

'Uh?' Chops' eyebrows curl over in disbelief.

'Only for an hour or two. You won't notice he's been away.'

'You must be off your head, mun. What's this for, a dog show or something?'

Chops is studying Jim's face now. The eyebrows are focusing in.

'Not exactly.'

'Tell me what you want him for or you can forget it.'

When Jim tells him, Chops erupts into laughter. The blood-splattered smock draped around his rotund stomach heaves up and down with convulsions. He stares hard at Jim once again, then gets up and gazes through the dusty window which faces the back yard. 'One hundred pounds!' he says with a note of triumph in his voice and without turning round.

'Whaat?' exclaims Jim. 'I'm only borrowing him, not buying him. What do you think I'm going to do, melt him down to make gold ingots?'

One pint down the line, Brian and Gary wait in the pickup for Jim to arrive. They've glazed over and drifted into a soundless limbo. From where they sit, the street ahead is almost straight and level, then it drops dramatically, dicing the roofs either side into giant steps which descend out of sight, while the road heads towards the sky. The sky is pierced by tangerine shafts of dying sunlight which ricochet off the roofs of the houses into their eyes.

'It's a good sunset,' suggests Gary, to break the silence.

'What do you think you are, a bloody artist or something?'

Gary flinches. 'No, but my father was. Still is, I suppose.'

'A piss artist, if you ask me.'

'No, he was a real artist,' insists Gary, indignant and defensive. 'I seen some of his pictures. They're tidy.'

Brian scoffs. 'Got pissed, put your mother in the club, then buggered off.'

Gary can't say any more. It's as if Brian has got two metal rods and is twirling them about in his intestine. They lapse back into an uneasy silence.

There's a knock on the window. Jim and Chops have emerged from the shop. Chops looks incongruous with the silly hat on his head, holding a quivering mass of light-brown fur in his out-sized pink hands. Brian reaches out to open the door and Chops literally throws the dog onto the seat. It recovers quickly, uncurls itself and sits up, looking a little dazed. Chops has gone back for something now. Jim gently sweeps the dog off the seat so that it lands in a tangled mop round the gearstick. He closes the pickup door and winds down the window. Chops re-emerges with one of those squeaky bags full of some unidentified blood-ridden meat.

'I'd better throw it in the back. Tiger will kill for this,' he explains, then points an admonishing finger at his dog, who cowers on the floor at Gary's feet. 'You behave now, right?'

Jim drives the pickup down Rhiwfelin and out of Tairffynnon towards Brynbedw, casting occasional glances at his temporary acquisition. Tiger looks remarkably like the late Tricksy, but he's more lively and apparently not bothered in the least about being in strange company. On the floor of the cab, he prances about and spins round and round for some time, then he puts his front paws on Gary's leg and looks lovingly up at him, juddering all over, his tail wagging furiously. Gary tries hard not to have hateful thoughts about him.

'I think he likes you,' says Jim.

'Yeah, a hell of a lot,' says Brian with a leer.

'*Ych*, gerroff!' Gary pushes the dog into a heap under the dashboard and keeps it at bay with his foot.

Time is running short when they pull into River View. It's nearly dark and the Bowdens are due back very soon. John and Gwyn have finished and gone home in John's car. The neighbours have returned over the road, so they have to be careful. Brian retrieves Tricksy's corpse from behind a bush. Hurriedly, they remove the collar from around its neck and put it on Tiger. Then Jim quietly unlocks the front door, throws Tiger a good few yards in and shuts it quickly. Immediately, they can hear barking through the door.

Chops has instructed Jim to lay a trail from right by the front door. While Brian and Gary watch bemused, he recovers the plastic bag from the back of the pickup, empties some of the bloodied contents into his hand and begins to drag them down the steps, then turns towards the hedge. Amazingly, Tiger can already smell it from indoors. His bark turns to a frantic yelp and he starts scratching at the base of the door. As Jim heads towards the hedge, Gary starts to panic that the Bowdens are going to return.

'Come on please Jim,' he whines. 'They're going to come back, I know they are.'

'Shaddup and quit moaning,' snaps Brian. With painful slowness, Jim drags the meat the last few yards and deposits the vile substance in its bag in the hedge. 'Right, let's go.'

They dump the dead dog in the back of the pickup, leap in and head off down the road to park it in the quarry layby. The trap has been laid. All they have to do now is return to the field side of the hedge to receive Tiger, alias Tricksy.

Brian is staying put. 'You and Gary can go. I think you're bloody mad.' He puts his feet up on the dashboard and folds his arms determinedly.

Gary is happy to go with his boss. Everything is an adventure with Jim. It's getting quite dark now. They scale an old wooden gate which is practically falling apart, and crouched, they follow the roadside hedge. This is in a dip, so they can't be seen from another house. Gary's heart is thumping as they shuffle along. He's enjoying this enormously. Upon reaching the spot in the hedge, they scrabble about for some time until Jim finds the meat. Now all they have to do is await the return of the Bowdens.

'It's cold,' says Gary, sitting on the side of the hedge, huddled up, starting to regret this adventure, 'and dark. I hope they aren't long.'

'They won't be.' Jim takes out a packet of mints and offers one to Gary. They stay silent for a few minutes, then Jim says: 'I got lost once, in the dark, when I was a kid. Right up on the mountains.'

Gary imagines a miniature Jim out on the moonlit mountain, wolves howling.'Aaaaaaooooooh!' Wolves? Maybe not. He pulls his coat round him tighter. 'How did you come to be lost on the mountain?'

'My parents and another family, we went for a day's outing up to the mid-Wales mountains in my dad's Zephyr. We had a picnic and went for a walk, things like that.'

'And ...?'

'I went for a wander on my own. A bit of a mist came down and I got completely lost. Whichever way I turned, it all looked the same: heather and peat bogs trailing off into the mist. By the time the mist cleared, it was getting dark, and cold, though there was a moon out. I'd walked and walked and I was hopelessly lost.'

'What did you do?' Gary is up there on those mountains, a lost look on his face.

'I got more and more cold and tired. In the end, I curled up in a ball on the ground and cried and cried.'

Gary is quite taken aback that Jim is admitting to this. He's also quite surprised. He was expecting Jim to have come up with some brilliant plan to find his way back.

'How old where you?'

'Ten-ish I suppose. I don't remember exactly.'

'So what happened? Did they get the helicopters out?'

Jim laughs. 'Not in those days. No, after I'd been curled up for some time, getting even more cold and damp, I got this odd feeling and I looked up.'

Electric waves are passing over Gary's head. 'Yeah, what did you see?'

'There was a man stood there about five yards away. A really wild old bugger. I stood up straight away. He was just standing there. He got this long wild hair and a rough beard.'

'What was he dressed like?'

'Oh, a cap, rough shirt, waistcoat, trousers, boots. He was really shabby. Even in the moonlight, you could see his clothes were really dirty with holes and bits hanging off. He smelt. Boy he smelt bad. It got right in your mouth.' He reaches in his pocket for another mint.

A car comes along the road from Felinwen. They pause for a moment, holding their breath, watching to see if it pulls into River View. It carries on past and they breathe again.

'So what did you do?' Gary asks, 'when you saw this man.'

'I wanted to bloody run. I can tell you, but he was my only hope of finding my way back, so I couldn't. I didn't say anything. He just beckoned, and I followed. He walked for about five minutes, over a rise, then along the side of a hill. I can still see him plodding along in front. He seemed quite big to me at the time, but he was probably only a little man. But he moved fast. I had to keep breaking into a trot to keep up with him. He was sure-footed too, like a goat. He never looked back to see if I was following him.

'Then what?'

'We came to a stream and I just knew if I followed it down, it would lead to the cars. I looked round to thank him, but he was nowhere to be seen. I never saw him again. Thinking back, he never said a single word to me.'

'So did you get back ok?'

'I just followed the stream down and in no time, I came to the clearing where the cars were. Mum was there with Aunty Jill and some of the locals. Dad was up the mountain with a search party.'

Funny to hear Jim saying 'Dad' and 'Mum' and 'Aunty Jill'.

'Who was the old boy then?'

'That's the funny bit, not a word of a lie …' Another car is coming down the road. They tense up. The driver changes down to third, then second. Jim grabs the meat and gets ready. The car has stopped. The gates to River View are being opened. The car pulls in with a sgrunch of gravel. Jim and Gary are both straining to look through the hedge now. They can hear some chattering and fairly bad-tempered muttering, then the outside light goes on. They duck down and keep still.

Now the front door is being opened. Instantly, Tiger darts through and starts snuffling his way past the Bowdens, down the steps and across to the hedge.

'Tricksy darling,' says Mrs Bowden.

'Where's he off to?' Mr Bowden follows him.

Tiger's progress is painfully slow. Jim and Gary are willing him to come towards them. Now Mr Bowden is running after him. He's going to pick him up.

'Hello Tricksy,' he says, grasping him in his arms with a sickly affectionate look on his face.

'Leave him darling, he's probably going to do his business,' chimes Mrs Bowden.

'Oh no!' thinks Jim, there goes his £5,000. And what's he going to say to Chops?

'Ow! Ow! Bloody dog!' Tiger has bitten Mr Bowden's hand and run free. Mr Bowden is jumping up and down, nursing his right hand with his left.

'Bloody, bloody dog!'

'Darling, what's the matter?'

'He's bitten me. I can't believe it. Tricksy's bitten me.'

'Better to leave him to do his business dear, and come in the house.'

'I'll give him business.'

As they go in, Tiger climbs the hedge, heading straight for Jim's hand and the miracle meat.

When they get back to the pick-up, Tiger is still devouring the obscene substance. Every time he is moved, or anyone comes near, he growls dangerously. Jim very delicately takes the collar off him, then takes it to the back of the pickup to put it back on the late Tricksy. Then he takes Tricksy by the scruff of the neck, walks down to the road and disappears into the darkness. When he returns, minus Tricksy, Gary asks excitedly: 'Are we going to stage the accident now then?'

'No way,' says Jim, looking distastefully at his hands, wishing he could wash them. 'Tricksy's cold and starting to go stiff. They'd see he's been dead a while. We don't want them to find him yet. If they don't find him for a while, there'll be no telling when he was killed.'

They jump into the pickup, and Jim sits back with a satisfied gleam on his face. 'I think this calls for a drink. Got any money, Brian?'

'Whaat? Brian looks daggers.'

'Only joking.' Jim takes a roll of notes out of his top pocket. 'Time to celebrate.'

It's Saturday morning, and Jim is being carried along by a large wave of optimism, as well as his dented Porsche, towards River View. Admittedly, he was a fool to let the dog out, he thinks, but all that has been sorted out now and it might just work to his advantage. The loss of his precious dog might just soften Mr Bowden a little for once. He's approaching the last bend now, and he notes that Tricksy's corpse has gone, and, sure enough, as he pulls into River View, there's Mr Bowden wielding a spade and making a hole on the edge of the lawn. As Jim hops out of his car, he observes that the old man's face looks drained and weary, with more than a trace of red round the eyes.

'What are you doing? Planting a tree?' asks Jim cheerily.

'No,' says Mr Bowden, every word a dead weight, 'we lost our dog last night.'

'I'm sorry to hear that. Was he ill then?'

'No, it looks as if he was struck down by a car. They didn't even have the decency to tell us. Mind you, it might have been late at night. We didn't find his little body until this morning.'

'Oh dear, that's very sad,' says Jim, looking suitably sympathetic.

'It's such a pity we parted on bad terms,' says Mr Bowden, looking down at the battered corpse lying a few feet away on the grass. 'He bit me you know.' He holds out a bandaged hand as evidence. 'Perhaps he was angry that we left him. Anyhow, we shall never know.'

Jim nods gravely. Mr Bowden changes the subject. 'Your men did a good job, however, left no mess either. And the flashing's been done too.'

'Yes of course.' Jim looks suitably modest.

'I think I owe you some money, don't I?'

Jim can't believe what he's hearing. He didn't even have to ask. He can already feel the crisp cheque warming the inside of his wallet. His face adopts a 'Call me Jim the reliable' expression.

'You'd better come inside.'

Just then, a car pulls up into their entrance splay. A bright red Escort. A man steps out looking very perturbed and walks tentatively through the gate. He sees the hole in the ground and looks up at Mr Bowden.

'It looks like I've got the right place,' he says. 'I didn't sleep a wink last night. I'm afraid I've got a confession to make.'

'Oh yes?'

'I was driving past here yesterday afternoon, and I hit a dog down.'

'Yesterday afternoon?' Mr Bowden looks puzzled. 'What time?'

I was in a desperate hurry to pick the nippers up from school, so it must have been about half-past three. '

'Is this the dog you hit?' He points at Tricksy's sad remains.

'Yeah, that's him alright.'

'But that doesn't make sense, he was alive when we saw

him at five, and in the house ...' He steps back hurriedly as a silver Porsche brushes past him and disappears down the road in a cloud of exhaust fumes.

3

HUGHES THE FUSE

Hafn Derwen is a row of sombre dwellings set into a dramatic gorge of grey cliffs, which frown at each-other over a fast-moving river. You can buy a postcard of the village in the post office, taken on a summer's day with soft, billowy clouds and sunlight sparkling on the water. But you should see the place now, with torrential hail sweeping down from the darkness, whipping across the street-lit roofs and strafing the surface of the water.

Downstream, where the gorge opens out a little, a dazzling halogen lamp pinpoints an isolated property between the river and the rock face. There's a muddy yard full of sodden timbers, a garage of corrugated sheets bulging with building materials, which rattles noisily in the hail, and a rusted old JCB in the corner of the garden.

The house has been built of leftovers from various jobs. The front roof is asbestos-slated and the back roof is concrete-tiled. Some windows are in hardwood, some softwood, some PVC. Framed in one of those windows, his features distorted by the wet glass, you can see Jim at his desk pricing a job, his fingers thumping away at a calculator.

The phone rings. He writes down a figure hurriedly, then answers it. 'Mr Isiah, it's good to hear from you,' he says without conviction, then he grimaces and holds the receiver away from his ear for a moment. 'No, your bungalow will definitely be ready by Christmas. Guaranteed.' There's a further verbal barrage and Jim flinches again. 'It will be,' he says, gesticulating at the phone with his open palm, 'No problem.' Suddenly, his face adopts a hunted look. 'Ok,' he says hesitantly, 'I'll agree to that, but it makes no difference, because it'll be done anyway.' He stares with surprise at the receiver and puts it down. The caller has hung up on him.

'Oh no, what have you promised him now?' Beryl slouches through the door, a picture of weariness. Jim's boundless energy seems to drain his wife rather than boost her. She wears a hang-dog look, emphasised by her hollow cheeks, the long cardigan, the mid-calf length skirt and the well-trodden slippers. She holds a lit cigarette in her hand, but rarely seems to puff at it; it just makes her blink a lot and fills the air with acrid smoke. 'I've told you to watch that man.' She sighs.

The phone rings again and the fax machine bursts into life, making space-alien noises. Alun escapes from under his mother's arms and runs over to it. At six, he's a miniature version of his dad, but with fair hair and sky-blue eyes.

'Cor, wicked, whassis? It sounds well cool.'

'It's a fax machine.' Jim looks worriedly at it. It's printing out now.

'Wassat for?'

'It's for sending letters and things down the phone.'

'Coo-ul. Don't they get crumpled up?' The print-out finishes and a hidden guillotine chops the paper noisily off the roll. Beryl reaches forward and grabs the letter. She absorbs its contents, gasps with disbelief and stares despairingly at Jim.

'How could you agree to this?' She prods the paper with an angry finger.

'What's that darling?'

She reads: 'Dear Mr Davies, further to our telephone discussion, I confirm your agreement to knock £10,000 off the price of my bungalow if it isn't completed by Christmas. Yours sincerely, H. Isiah.'

'He must have had that letter ready,' says Jim with amazement. Beryl flicks it dismissively onto the desk and storms out of the room.

'It's Monday morning and three degrees below. Mr Isiah's bungalow and everything around it is covered in a sugary coating of frost, which sparkles in the early sun. Inside the site caravan, a gas fire hisses and splutters and the boys huddle round it drinking tea, reluctant to venture out. Gwyn paces back and fore like a caged animal, shaking everything. The narrow door opens and a wide Jim struggles in. 'It's a cold one boys,' he says unnecessarily. 'Never mind, you've got plenty to keep you warm. This job's got to be finished by Christmas.' He shuts the door behind him.

'No way, Jim.'

'Bullshit.'

'Dream on, pal.'

Jim looks unusually forlorn for a moment. 'If it isn't, you may be looking for a new boss.'

'Maybe you'd better look for some new slaves then,' Brian retorts, 'cos no way are we going to get this done by Christmas. Anyway, you're not ready for me and Gary to do plasterboarding yet.'

'Nor me to do plumbing neither,' adds Trevor.

'I don't care if you're ready or not, you'll have to do it.'

'What, you want me to clip the pipes onto fresh air?'

'Do whatever you have to, just get the job finished by Christmas.'

Gwyn looks Jim in the eye. 'What's the matter, awkward customer?'

'You could say that.'

Gwyn scratches the back of his neck for a moment and looks pensive. 'I reckon it should be possible in a month, provided it's planned properly mind.'

'Maybe you're right,' says Trevor, staring thoughtfully into his tea. 'Along with a bit of healthy persuasion, like.'

Jim looks puzzled. 'What kind of persuasion?'

'A few of the old spondoolies,' says Brian, rubbing his thumb and forefinger together. 'A bonus.'

Jim adopts that hard-done-by look that always accompanies any suggestion of him parting with money. 'Ok,' he grunts, 'a hundred quid each to finish before Christmas.'

'Five hundred,' counters Brian, stony-faced.

Jim stiffens. 'Two hundred then,' he concedes grudgingly, 'and I'm an idiot to give you that. Right, get on with it. I'm going before I change my mind.' He bolts out of the door and bounds through the biting cold air back to his car.

Externally, the bungalow has been roofed and windowed, but inside it's still an empty shell: no partitions, no ceiling. There's still a lot to do.

'Right, let's get a mix,' says Gwyn. 'We're all going to lay blocks today.' He opens the caravan door and hurls out the dregs of his tea.

'All?'

'All. Then we'll all plasterboard. Where's Oar?'

'Oar? Who's Oar?' asks Brian, puzzled.

'He's the new labourer.'

'Why's he called Oar?'

Byron smiles. 'Probably because he's long and thin. You obviously haven't seen him. He's out there, trying to start the mixer. Take a look.'

Oar is indeed very tall and thin with an ugly, squashed face and ripped clothes. He looks as if some malignant giant has picked him up and stretched him, just for a laugh, then dropped him on the ground and stamped on him, before losing interest, enabling him to escape through a particularly dense thorn bush. He cranks away at the mixer with a spindly arm, but there's no response.

Byron comes over to help. In contrast to Oar, he's short and squat with a wide face and moustache. 'She'll have to be bump-started,' he says, with an encouraging smile.

'Uh?'

'Watch me,' says Byron, pushing Oar aside, 'and learn.' He stands two pieces of upright timber opposite one another in the upturned bowl of the mixer, then lays a plank on edge across the top, jamming it between the two uprights.

'Yeah, wassat for? Lot of good that is, innit?'

Byron smiles patiently. 'You grab one end of the plank and I grab mine.'

'Then what?'

'Then we run round and round.'

'Uh?'

By now, a group of spectators has gathered. Fuelled by verbal abuse, the two run in a circle and the bowl churns reluctantly round. Oar trips and falls headlong, just as the motor bursts into life. The plank begins revolving fast, still attached to the mixer, which has become a kind of crude helicopter. There's a burst of applause.

'Get a move on,' barks Brian,' addressing Oar's prostrate body. 'We need a mix. You're not paid to lie about all day.' Oar gets shakily to his feet, oblivious of the rotating plank. As he rises, it catches him on the back of the neck, felling him like a tree. He lies there twitching, occupying a remarkable length of ground.

'That does it,' says Brian. 'Dock his wages.'

When he walks into Mr Isiah's bungalow for a second time, Hughes the Fuse is certain that something is up. Everyone is fitting door linings. A few days before, everyone was laying blocks and that skinny labourer was actually running with the wheelbarrow. What's more, Gwyn tells him: 'Mark all the switches and sockets and we'll help you out with the back boxes.'

'What's going on here?'

'Nothing.'

'You've never been in this much of a hurry before, I can smell a bonus.'

Gwyn looks blank.

'If you're getting a bonus, I want a slice of the action.' Jim's electrician is small in stature, but he makes up for his size with an aggressive streak. Most people are wary of him, but Gwyn couldn't care less. 'You're on a price, pal. The faster you work, the more you earn. If you don't want the job, push off and we'll get someone else.'

Hughes says nothing, but as he begins to lay out the cables, a great knot of resentment begins to seethe and fester in his gut. Dark thoughts gather and breed. He plots his revenge. Nobody gets the better of him. Nobody gains at his expense. They might push someone else around, but they're not going to make a fool of John Hughes. He snips viciously at the wires, sending offcuts in all directions.

Now as he begins to clip cable down the partitions, he can't help noticing that the upper blocks have not long been laid. He steals a Machiavellian grin. All he has to do is hit the clip in nice and hard, 'Bang! Bang!' The top block comes loose. He does the same with the next drop, and the next.

Several rooms later, he pipes up in his high-pitched voice, 'How am I supposed to fix cables when all these blocks are loose?'

'What blocks?'

'These top blocks. They're all loose.'

That'll delay them, re-bedding that lot, thinks Hughes. That'll delay them good and proper.

He's pulling cables down now, near the corner of a plasterboard sheet. If he just yanks the cable a bit roughly … perfect. The whole corner rips off and dangles down, shedding white powder. 'You've got some rubbish plasterboarding here. This piece has come off in my hands.'

Two points to Hughes. But here's a good one! He's marked out all the kitchen sockets in the wrong place. A silly mistake! He chuckles to himself. All because they've rushed him. He can hear them now, disc-cutting and chiselling away at the blockwork. All that wasted effort. All that dust assaulting their lungs, to no purpose. He smirks. He's beginning to enjoy this. He can hear drilling now. They're fixing in the boxes. A complete waste of time. He listens intently, counting each hole drilled. There are seven sockets, a cooker point, a fridge spur, two light switches, a TV point. That's twenty-four holes.

As they near number twenty-four, Hughes appears at the

kitchen door. He holds the electrical drawing in his hand with a hugely apologetic look on his face. 'You're not going to believe this, boys.'

Gwyn looks up, that bovine look, drill in hand. 'Yeah, what?'

'I've gone and read the kitchen on the plan the wrong way round. All these sockets here, they're meant to be over on the opposite wall. Sorry about that.'

Gwyn picks up a back-box to throw at him, but Hughes is protected by an invisible shield: the electrics have to be done. They are at his mercy. He basks and wallows in his new-found power. He shrugs. 'You're rushing me, see. I know you're all in a hurry to get this finished, just for Jim's sake, but that's how mistakes are made. The light switches can stay, though. That's something, isn't it?'

We're in the living room now. 'It's kind of weird this room,' says Gary. 'All these curved walls and arches and things.' Mr Isiah's living room certainly is unusual. An apse that's semi-circular on plan with curved alcoves has been built at the far end like a stage set, with solid curved seating all round and a central arched window. The whole of this is raised on a dais, making the ceiling quite low. Expensive new slate slabs are being laid on the raised area.

Oar takes a run-up with a battered wheelbarrow, which squeaks its way up a plank to the higher level. Compo slops over the sides.

'This mix is too wet! And it's too rich,' growls Gwyn. 'Take it back and put more sand in it.' Oar sulks for as long as he dares, then makes off again with the full barrow.

'I reckon it makes a tidy feature,' says Trevor, as he marks out one of the slabs, approximating the curve to a series of straight lines. 'It looks like part of a castle or something. By rights, these walls should be in stone.'

'It'll make a good dining area,' says Byron, tapping down a slab with the handle of his lump hammer. Isiah is bringing something soon, isn't he, to go in here. Maybe it's a marble table.'

'It could be a fountain or something,' suggests Gary.

Brian reflects for a moment. 'No, it looks like the kind of alcove you get in nightclubs. It's a bar, that's what's going in the middle,' he decides, 'a curved bar. A bar would be tidy in here.'

'There's no water supply anyway,' says Trevor, 'so I doubt it's a fountain or a bar.' He switches on the disc cutter and it bites into the stone, screaming and obliterating everything in clouds of choking dust. Seconds later, it goes off again and slowly grinds to a halt. 'Oh no, don't tell me it's packed up!' He twists it on its side and stares hopelessly at it.

A small, stroppy figure emerges through the haze. 'I've turned the power off. I can't be expected to work in all this dust. You'll have to cut outside.'

'It's pissing with rain, Hughes.'

'That's your problem.'

'No, it's yours. Wear a mask.'

'I'm not prepared to discuss the matter further. If you want me to complete the wiring, you have to provide me with an acceptable working environment.'

'Acceptable working environment,' mimics Oar.

'Do as he asks,' says Gwyn, looking dangerous.

John is tiling the bathroom. The Isiahs have chosen a sort of slime green. 'This colour is turning my stomach,' he remarks, fixing the last tile onto the pipe boxing at the side of the bath.

Hughes has been standing at the door, resting his shoulder against the frame, putting his weight on one leg and watching John finish off. When he's good and ready, he says, 'You do realise that the pipes have to be earth bonded.'

'The pipes have been boxed in. It's too late.'

Hughes folds his arms and raises his chin, adopting a superior attitude which he is in the process of perfecting. 'The pipes have to be earthed for safety reasons. You don't want anyone getting electrocuted, do you?'

'Not just anyone,' replies John.

This goes over Hughes' head. 'I'm sorry, but I can't certify that the system is safe until the pipes have been properly earth bonded. Until then there can be no power.' He says this as if he's depriving them of ice-cream. 'You do realise my position, don't you?'

'Still standing so far,' mutters John. 'Perhaps you could explain,' he adds, 'why you are telling me now and not before the pipes were boxed in.'

'Well, you should check on these things before racing ahead, shouldn't you?'

John doesn't say a word. He picks up a claw hammer and rips at the tiles he's just laid, tearing them off the ply so that they clatter on the floor in a sticky heap. Then he hacks at the corner of the boxing and yanks away a large sheet, exposing the pipes. 'There you are, bond your bloody pipes.'

'Oh no,' says Hughes, 'not here. The earth cable is on the other side, beneath this piece of boxing here.'

It's breaktime in the caravan a few days later and most of the boys are reading their tabloids. Gary is staring at his feet. He's noticed that if he moves his toes, his boots make facial expressions at him. He can get them to register anger, surprise, even amusement. He sets them on edge and gets them to converse with one another.

A vehicle pulls up on site. 'Who is it, Gary?' asks Brian.

'GARY!'

'Uh?'

'Who is it?'

Gary leans forward and peers out of the window. Sleet has started driving in from the east. It spatters the glass, gradually obscuring his vision. 'It's a big white van. A bloke in a long coat is getting out. He's going into the bungalow.'

'Bloody hell, he'll be here next. Can't he see it's break-time?' They sit back in their seats, keeping a low profile, hoping not to be seen.

'He's coming this way now. He's coming to the caravan.' They try hard to merge with the upholstery.

The door opens, revealing a man in a heavy brown coat, with a hood pulled over his head and a long biblical beard. There's something disturbingly grey about his face, and those eyes, they're jet black, like looking into two bottomless pits. He's wearing a male perfume, which clings. A man in a boiler suit hovers behind him.

'Sorry to bother you.'

The boys yawn and stretch as if they've been woken from a deep slumber.

'I wonder if you'd be so good as to give us a hand.' He says this in such a way that even Brian can't fob him off.

In the back of the van are several large dark grey slabs of carved slate with angle fixings at the corners and pieces of cardboard protecting the edges. 'Careful now, gentlemen.' The slabs are back-breakingly heavy. Mr Isiah doesn't lift a finger to help. Grumpily, they slither through the fallen sleet and struggle in with the first four. He supervises their positioning on the dais of the apse in the living room. As they're raised on edge, the man in the blue boiler suit bolts them together to form a rectangular box on stubby legs, which he adjusts at the base.

The last slab is the heaviest. It's for the top. It has to go on its side through the doors, but once into the living room, they carry it flat, with Oar on the long side, approaching the dais backwards. He looks overstressed, sinews humming. Any second, some part of him is going to burst or snap horrifically. He fails to climb the step, half-stumbles, and in dreadful slow motion, the slab sinks onto the floor of the dais, pinning him under it. The only parts of him visible are a pair of legs from the knee downwards, which flail about pathetically, a head, which shakes from side to side, opening and shutting its mouth like a fish and the fingers of two hands, which push frantically upwards on the slab.

'I think he's squashed his rowlocks,' quips Brian.

'He's Oar-izontal,' says Gary.

'Gwyn looks down and addresses the head, which is beginning to turn a funny colour. 'You stay there now. Don't move. We'll get this slab off you now. Just give us a breather.'

This time, even Mr Isiah gives a hand. When the slab has finally been raised, measured and manoeuvred into position, he dismisses the boys. 'Thank you for your help. I'm sure you'll want to get back to your break now.'

But as soon as he's gone in the big van, they rush back in and swarm all over the object, studying it closely. All four sides are engraved in swirling Celtic patterns. The top is plain, apart from a groove around the perimeter. It overhangs the sides by about six inches. The slate is polished: a dark, colourless grey.

Trevor peers under the top slab. 'It's definitely not a table, you can't get your legs underneath. There's not enough overhang.'

'It's an altar,' says John. 'I'd have thought that was obvious.'

'Looks more like a tomb to me,' says Gary. 'It looks bloody depressing. I didn't like the look of that bloke,' he screws up his nose, 'maybe he's with one of those funny religions, them cults like.'

'Sure to be,' says Byron, with a look of worried sincerity.

'I wonder what the altar's for?' Even Gwyn looks apprehensive. He rubs the palm of his hand thoughtfully across the polished surface.

'Bound to be for making sacrifices. Look,' says Brian. 'See this groove by here, that's for catching blood, so it doesn't spill over the sides. They'll slip on their arses on these slabs if it goes on the floor. It doesn't look good if they're in the middle of chanting something and they hit the deck.'

'What will they sacrifice?' asks Oar. He looks a bit peaky after being crushed under the slab. 'Not humans?'

'There's no depends,' says Brian, who appears to have become an expert on the subject. 'Sheep maybe. Goats is a favourite. Aye, or maybe humans.'

'Don't joke,' pipes up Hughes in his shrill voice, 'It's no laughing matter. These things happen, terrible things, which people don't know about.' He shivers. 'And there's forces, dark forces. I've seen a programme on the telly.'

'Yes and there's currents,' adds Gwyn, 'invisible currents that go through wires in the walls and make things work. We need them now.'

'I'm doing my best,' says Hughes, wandering off. 'Don't pressurise me. It doesn't pay to push me.'

Strong vibes of hate follow his retreating back.

Gary's mum sits on a stool in their back kitchen. She's got a craving for something, but for a second, she's forgotten what. Unwashed pots and pans, crockery and cutlery are strewn over the worktops all around her. A cat stands on the draining board, licking at this morning's cereal bowl. A fag! She remembers with a sigh. She's given up. She picks up a nail file and starts sawing away at her fingernails.

Gary is rummaging in the fridge. 'Mum, is there anything to eat, I'm bloody starving!'

'You're always hungry. What's the matter with you? Have you got worms or something?'

'Mum, I've just done a day's work. It's normal to be hungry after you've been working.'

'Well go into town and get some chips.' She waves the nailfile dismissively at him.

'I'll faint before I get there.'

She hops down from the stool. 'Alright, sit down. I'll get you something. I'm starting to feel peckish myself. Not like me.'

The doorbell rings. She rushes out. Gary throws his hands up in despair. She opens the door. Brian is standing there. She eyes him up and down approvingly, like livestock at a mart.

He coughs. 'Hello Sheila. I've brought the troops.' Gwyn, John and the others hover at the doorstep behind him, rubbing their hands with the cold.

'Come in all of you, they're ready. I hope they're alright.' She leads them into the side room, which is a sea of material, curtains and items of clothing she's making for customers. Her sewing machine, like a sinking liner, barely stays afloat among it all. She searches about under things and behind chairs and eventually emerges with a wide, flat cardboard box.

'D'you want to try them on?'

'No,' says Gwyn hurriedly, 'I'm sure they're alright.' He reaches into his pocket and pulls out some notes.

'No, I'm not going to charge you boys. You're Gary's mates.' She starts to back off.

'Don't be daft, Sheila, it's cost you time and money.' He presses the notes into her hand.

'When's the fancy dress do?'

'Tomorrow night.'

'Well, have a good time.'

The boys are assembled, in costume, in Mr Isiah's living room. 'Boy, that looks scary,' says Gary, looking at Brian's hooded cloak.

'Good, but I can't see through the eye slits,' says Brian worriedly. 'How am I going to read this stuff? And the light is dim. I'll have to make it up.'

John unwraps a small device from its polythene packet and pops it into his mouth. 'How does this sound?' His voice comes out gurgly as if he's speaking from a dank cave surrounded by frogs.

'*Ych a fi*, that's brilliant. Where did you get it from?'

'A toy shop in London.'

Presently, Gwyn whispers urgently, 'Quick, he's coming. Get your hoods on! You three, get in the hall cupboard now.'

Hughes has been summoned because something is tripping out the electrics, but as he walks in, he can see that lights are on in the hall. Maybe it's been sorted. If it has, he's going to have words with someone. 'Hello! Hello!' No sign of anyone. Wait! He can hear voices in the living room. He bursts through the door, then stops in his tracks. It's dark in there. The heavy purple curtains have been drawn and some candles lit in the alcoves of the apse. Maybe the fault is on this circuit. He strains his eyes to get used to the light. A strong smell of incense assaults his nostrils. There's another smell. He sniffs the air. He doesn't like it. What is it? Like a butcher's shop.

He senses movement at the far end and freezes. Two figures opposite one another on the stone seating in the apse rise to their feet and approach the altar. Even in the dim light, he can see that they're wearing full-length cloaks tied with cords round the middle. The heads are completely hooded with eye slits. He turns to run, but several pairs of hands grab him and more hooded figures drag him towards the dais. The door slams shut.

As he approaches the step, whimpering and protesting loudly, he glimpses a wooden table to one side, lit by a candelabra. On it is a bloodstained dagger with a nine-inch blade and what look like entrails and some dead furry creature. Next to it, on the floor, is an enamel bucket containing a dark liquid. He groans and struggles frantically as they take off his jumper and shirt and lift him onto the altar. They strap him down by the ankles and the chest.

His captors form a semi-circle round their prostrate victim. Hughes looks helplessly from one to the other, wondering what dark fate awaits him, and how soon it's going to happen. Presently, one of the figures begins reading from a black book, the words mumbled and slurred together, in a strange language. Hughes arches his back and writhes about in an effort to free himself. His hands shake violently.

'Who are you? What do you want from me?' He looks wild-eyed, like a trapped animal.

The figure on the right turns mechanically through ninety degrees, so that the eye-slits are trained on him. As he strains to lift his head, Hughes can see that he has a dagger in his hand, which he holds upwards, testing the blade. 'We are the followers of Nemnoc.' The voice has a strange gurgling quality. 'No doubt you will have heard of us.'

'Er … yes,' Hughes lies.

'Good. Good. We feast on the misdeeds of others and drink the blood of the weasel. Would you like to drink weasel's blood?' He asks with relish.

'There can't be much … I don't …'

The hooded head comes inches from Hughes' face and the blade of the dagger is pressed against his throat. 'Yes or no?'

'Yes, I've always wanted to …'

'Good, you shall, you shall. But first you must confess your misdeeds. I hope there are many. It would be a pity if we tire of you.'

The gurgling voice resumes. It sounds impatient, barely in control. 'Were you wicked as a child? Were you? Were you?'

Hughes thinks frantically. 'I kicked my brother's sandcastle over and told him my sister had done it. He punched her in the nose, and it bled …'

'Good, good! The grotesque hoods nod with approval. 'But a mere titbit! We hunger. Give us more. Feed us.'

'I used to pull the legs off grasshoppers, then leave them go.' He glances expectantly at his captors. They look unmoved.

'A crumb! A mere crumb! More! We are losing patience.'

Hughes is thinking desperately. The cat! Thank God! He remembers the cat. 'When I was little, our cat scratched me, so I put it in the washing machine and watched it go round and round. Then I took it out and put it in the freezer. I could hear it clawing at the door. I forgot about it then; but that afternoon, I went in for a lolly and it dropped out. Clunk! Onto the floor. It was frozen solid. I was sorry about what I'd done, so I put it in the oven to melt, but it wouldn't come back to life.' He looks pathetically for their approval.

Their spokesman seems pleased. 'An excellent starter! A tasty morsel!' Hughes looks relieved. Maybe they'll let him go now. But the hood creeps up close again, and a clammy voice asks: 'I hope you weren't a good boy at school.'

Hughes doesn't need prompting this time. 'I hated my teacher. She always picked on me.' He pouts.

'So what did you do? Did you punish her? Did you?'

He nods. When nobody was looking, I sneaked a lot of pills in her tea that I nicked from my grandad. She went all green, then sicked up all over the floor. They found pills in the sick, then there was a big witch hunt to find who was guilty. I dropped some pills I had left into Philip Rees' pocket and left an anonymous note saying he'd done it. That was because he wouldn't let me copy something before from his exercise book. He got the cane for that.'

'A spicy dish! And garnished with pure wickedness! Now bring us a dessert of just deserts!'

'My boss was a stupid old fool.' Hughes sneers. 'I'm an electrician, you see. He never paid me enough, so I played tricks on him and changed cables round. He couldn't understand why everything went wrong. He thought he was going senile. Then one day, he docked my wages because I came in late.'

'Tell us how you got even with him.' They crowd around eagerly. Hughes hesitates. He daren't not tell them, but what if it gets out? He could always say he made it up. He could always say that.

'He was up a ladder fixing an outside light and he kept shouting and shouting for me to turn on the mains. Then after that, he changed his mind and told me to leave it off. Well, I didn't hear the last bit did I? I switched on like he said and had him a real belter! He fell from the ladder straight into a bush and flattened it. "You asked me to switch on the mains!" I told him. He damaged his hip. He wasn't long retiring after that. I had the business off him cheap.'

'Absolutely delicious. He is one of us! He is truly one of us! He must be initiated.' They all nod their heads in agreement.

Hughes looks apprehensive and enquires tentatively, 'This initiation, what happens?'

'We brand you with the mark of Nemnoc and you drink the blood of the weasel. It is a great honour!'

'I want to be initiated,' says Hughes reluctantly, immensely relieved that they aren't going to cut anything off.

'Very well, then, you shall.' Almost at once they begin chanting, the same foreign words, over and over. Behind his hood, Oar has been struggling to keep control. Now he finally loses it. Seized by a fit of mirth, he bends double, clutching his stomach, shaking like a rag doll. 'The power has seized his organs!' gurgles John. 'He will recover.'

This sets Gary off. He begins to judder uncontrollably. John scolds him, 'You must be strong. Do not let the power take you.'

Bewildered, Hughes cranes his neck round nervously as a branding iron is now produced from behind him and held above his stomach. It smokes threateningly. The chanting increases in volume.

'Blindfold him! He must not see the mark of Nemnoc in reverse!' A piece of cloth is tied around his head. It presses against his eyeballs. In the darkness, Hughes waits in horrid suspense for the stinging pain. He's determined to show no reaction at all. That will impress them, he thinks. He won't make a sound.

'NOW!'

'Aaaaaaaaaaaaaaaaaaaaaaaaaaaaaaaaaaaaah!' They put a large wide plaster on the mark.

'This will heal the wound. See how you feel little pain? Do not remove it for four hours.' They're right, thinks Hughes. There's no pain. It's miraculous.

They take off the blindfold and the bonds round his chest. 'Sit him up.' A pewter goblet is brought forward. Hughes tries to forewarn his insides of the coming onslaught. He hopes there isn't much. He glances into the goblet. It's full! He groans inwardly.

The chanting starts again. Different words this time. Hands hold him steady. The goblet is held to his lips. 'Drink! This will give you speed and energy!'

Fighting back the urge to throw up, Hughes begins to drink. To his surprise, it tastes fine. A bit like tomato soup. He drinks it all. Weasel's blood indeed! If only people knew how silly these cults really were. Speed and energy! What speed and energy is a bit of tomato soup going to give him? When he's free, he's going to shop these idiots and sell his story to a newspaper for pots of money.

'Now you are one of us!' They untie the bonds round his ankles. 'Go. We will contact you. Tell no one of this!' Hardly believing his luck, Hughes slides off the altar, grabs his shirt and jumper, scampers like a rabbit out of the bungalow, leaps into his van and drives away.

'Right,' says Brian, 'let's clear this lot quick.'

'What a piece of slime,' says Gwyn, taking off his hood. 'Weasel is right.'

John removes the device from his mouth. 'He should be getting his speed and energy right now,' he says with a satisfied smile. 'I put a powerful laxative in his drink.'

Tairffynnon is looking half-heartedly festive as last-minute shoppers hurry to and fro, popping in and out of shops like nervous gerbils. A large Christmas tree has been placed outside the town hall, but half the lights have been broken by late-night revellers. A polystyrene fish and chip container is stuck in one of the branches. More lights have been draped back and fore across the High Street and a two-dimensional Father Christmas is hanging, slightly off plumb, from the first floor window of the toy shop.

Wet snowflakes are beginning to fall. Three middle-aged ladies huddle like sheep on the corner outside Woolworths.

'Are you ready for Christmas then?' asks one.

'Well, it all seems such a fuss, and in the end you wonder, what's the point of it all?' says another. They chorus in agreement.

'I don't think I'll bother with a turkey this year,' says a third. 'I told my husband, if he wants one, to buy it and cook it himself.'

'Ooh! What did he say?'

'He said it was a woman's job. It was EXPECTED of me, would you please.'

'What did you tell him, *bach*?'

'I told him, same as the turkey, to get stuffed.'

'Oooh!' They squeal with laughter, then turn their heads as a van comes grinding to a halt nearby and mounts the pavement. The door flies open and the driver rockets across the main road before plunging into the toilets.

'Well!' They put their hands to their mouths and snort with laughter. 'I wonder what he's been eating.'

'They've had a difference of opinion whatever it is.'

'I hope he's alright,' says the woman with a navy coat, looking with concern towards the door of the gents.

'D'you know him?'

'That's Hughes the electrician. My sister says he's a lovely man. A socket in the kitchen burnt out with her last year and he insisted on changing every socket in the house. He said he wasn't going to see her coming to any harm. Like a close friend to her he was.'

'Oh, bless him!'

'The old man he worked for, he had an accident, came off a ladder I think and damaged his hip. Hughes blamed himself for that, he said it was his fault. My sister told him not to be so daft.'

'It's types like that who blame themselves.'

'Yeah.'

It's snowing heavily as a police car scrunches into Mr Isiah's driveway. There must be half a dozen or so cars parked there, all turning a uniform white under a carpet of snow. The driver gets out. He's stiffly built with greying hair and a guarded look. He pans the property, drinking in every detail. Three officers get out and group quietly round him. They look apprehensive, constantly looking around them like birds feeding. The snow slides off their polished shoes.

'Remember, we're told there's at least one dagger and they're wearing cloaks. Watch for concealed weapons. When you approach any of them, make sure you can see both hands. You two, guard the back. Us two will try the front. If we ask for back-up, leg it in there.'

When the two policemen burst into the living room, Mr Isiah is standing at the altar with his back to the door. He wears a charcoal grey suit. The material has a bit of a shine to it and a little colony of dandruff nestles under the collar. His tall frame is straddled by large candles in pewter candlesticks, one each end of the altar. They flicker frantically with the sudden draught. In front of him, the curved seating in the apse is filled with a small congregation of happy people singing lustily from their song-sheets. Through the arched window at the back, the snowflakes fall relentlessly. With the hedge in the background, they're a pure white, but against the afternoon sky, they look like specs of dirty grey.

Hughes has taken off his shirt and he's standing by the wash-basin in his bathroom looking at the mirror. Across his stomach is a big wide plaster with sticky bits at both ends and cotton wool between. He pauses for a moment, summoning up the courage to take it off. He starts picking away at the corners and winces as it takes little hairs with it. He pulls at it quickly and one end comes away. Then, ever so slowly and nervously, he peels away the cotton wool. The skin isn't burnt at all. There's black lettering, a little smudged and the right way round as he views it in the mirror. There's an S then U ...

C... a bit of cotton wool is still stuck to the skin. He removes it carefully ... K ... E ... R.

It's getting dark and Tairffynnon is full of drunken people slithering about on the snowy streets. A year's inhibitions are being thrown to the wind. The Fox and Hounds contains an unbridled mass of heaving, swilling, laughing, swearing humanity. It's an addictive, heady place to be in. At a corner table, by a fake coal fire, which burns and never consumes, Jim's boys are on a high. They've finished the bungalow on time and they're waiting for their bonus. Nothing bothers them. When people come crashing and swaying into their table, they just hold their drinks and laugh it off.

'Here comes Father Christmas,' says Sue, looking towards the door.

Jim comes bounding in, dodging this way and that like a slalom skier to avoid people. He searches through the smoke and bedlam, spots his troops in the corner and fights his way to them. All eyes are riveted on the large brown envelope he holds in his hand. He rips it open and it gives birth to several smaller brown envelopes, which he passes around.

'What kept you, Jim?'

'I've been with the cops.'

'Drunk and disorderly?'

'No, the Isiahs were having their inaugural service and they had a raid. They've got their own little Christian group, the brothers and sisters of something. I forget the name of it,' he explains.

'A raid? Drugs?'

'You're not going to believe this.'

They pretend they don't know what's coming, rubbery expressions of expectancy on their faces.

'Hughes the Fuse fed the cops some bullshit about an evil cult ...'

'Yeah, carry on.'

'He said he looked in at the bungalow and there were hooded figures in there and ... it sounds so daft.'

'Come on, you can't half tell us.'

'He said they strapped him to the altar.'

They all laugh.

'And one of them had a big knife.' Jim looks embarrassed. 'He must have gone off his tree. They've cautioned him, I think. He started on again, but they kicked him out.'

'He went funny with us, didn't he?' says Brian, '... when that altar came. Talking about cults and things.' They all nod.

'Well, he convinced them at first.'

Jim goes to get a round and Brian homes in on Gary with a gurgling voice. 'Confess to me your secret thoughts.' Gary gets this odd feeling as if a powerful spotlight is being trained on him. He glances across and there's Sue looking straight at him with a million-dollar smile on her face, all for him. He flushes. 'I'd better not,' he thinks.

Gary is pinned to the bed. He can't move, and a hooded figure with eye-slits bends over him, holding a massive live cable next to his face. It spits and fizzes blue sparks.

'Confess!' says his tormentor, the high voice muffled behind the hood. 'Confess that you fancy Brian's girlfriend!' Gary raises his arms to tear off the hood. It comes apart with a swish to reveal a blinding light.

'Oh, you're awake,' says Gary's mum, opening his curtains.

Gary sits bolt upright in bed. 'Am I late for work?'

'It's Christmas Day, you dozy fool.' She gives him a hopeless smile.

He drops back onto the bed. 'Oh yeah, Merry Christmas.'

She stands, arms folded, by the window, sideways on, and looks out. 'Gary, come and look at this.'

'Mum, it's cold out there.'

'Come on.'

'Grumpily, he gets out of bed. His pyjamas are several sizes too small. He staggers over to the window, doubled up, shivering and scratching at his tummy between the buttons. 'What is it?'

'What do you see?'

'Snow, yeah wonderful.'

'What else?'

'I dunno, cars parked. Can I go back to bed now?'

'What about that one below the window?'

'Red Fiesta.'

She hands him a set of keys. 'It's yours.'

Gary's stunned. For a moment, he stops shivering. 'Don't be daft, Mum, you can't afford it.'

'Why do you think I've given up smoking? And there's my sewing and your dad helps me with money.'

Gary looks down at the floor. He's trying to put out of his mind that Christmas Eve when he was six and she came home late, drunk, with that smarmy accountant and Father Christmas never called.

'Thank-you, Mum. I don't know what to say. We can drive to Aunty Jean's in it later on.'

4

ALWAYS LOOK A GIFT HORSE IN THE MOUTH

Gary's driving up the coast road in the pickup. He's working, but not working. Jim has sent him to open some house for the grant inspector because the old dear is away. He's looking for a rusted Dutch barn on the right, a large white house and an old milk stand on the left. Here it is. He turns off at the milk stand onto a minor road with a central grass strip. The hedges close right in, almost choking the pickup. Gary's searching for another left turn, the third one off this road. This is it. A bumpy lane. And there's the house, fifty yards away, looking straight at him.

It's almost uncanny the way the house seems to actually be looking at him. But unlike his boots, which he can distort with his feet, the expression doesn't change. What is it? A kind of timid fear? The building has such a strong physical presence, you can almost reach out and touch it. Gary approaches slowly down the pot-holed lane, averting its gaze. He imagines telling the boys, 'This house I went to, it was looking at me, honest now, like it had got a face.'

'Shut up Gary. Hey did you hear what this pillock said?'

'Did you look round the back, Gary, maybe it's got an arse too.'

The house is two-storeyed, with a pair of Victorian sash windows each side of a roughly central door and a smaller, higher pair tucked right under the eaves. The front is limewashed white, but parts have flaked off, revealing a whole shade card of different colours beneath. The woodwork is painted in red and cream.

The roof is of old, heavy slates, half-cemented over, the surface a series of waves which sweep up to the chimneys at each end. Attached to the left-hand gable is a lower 'cegin fach', an old wash-house extension with its separate outside door and huge chimney.

Gary pulls onto the front yard, which is bounded by limewashed dry-stone walls with a large sycamore tree in one corner. The grant man hasn't arrived yet. He switches off the engine and gets out of the pickup. As he does so, an almost tangible peace descends on him like a veil. The sun flickers on his face through the branches of the tree. A gentle breeze comes in over the rocky fields, combing back the grass. It's the only sound. In the distance is a strip of sea, a flash of blue.

Ten minutes of sitting on the wall, half-basking, half-shivering in the sun and Gary decides to enter the house for a look around. He goes to the pickup, reaches for the keys and tries each one in turn on the front door. But as he inserts the third key, the door opens of its own accord and he walks into a narrow hall.

'It's surprisingly warm in the house. Gary creeps down the passageway, feeling like a burglar. At the far end, by the stairs, there's a door either side. He pauses. Left or right? Right. He opens the door, but suddenly conscious of his dirty boots, stops short of entering, hanging from the latch as if there was a deep pool of water he nearly stepped into.

He sees a musty, little-used parlour, all lace, china and polished surfaces. The suite is covered in white sheets. An old watercolour above the fireplace catches his attention: an ancient temple with shepherds in eastern clothing in the foreground. And on the table he notices a white marble bust of a man with a large beard and a pronounced forehead.

'Hello, young man,' comes a voice from behind him. Gary freezes, petrified. This must be a ghost. How do you behave with ghosts? Do you act natural, ignore them or what?

'Hello,' he says, acting cool, not daring to look round. He wonders if it's visible. He knows from the voice that it's an old lady. Maybe it's a skeleton, with putrescent skin hanging off it. Any second now, the bust will probably fly off the table and dash him to the ground.

'It's alright, *bach*. I'm not a ghost.'

Gary looks round, then down, and sees a little old lady wearing a check pinny standing in the opposite doorway. Her face is a mass of lines, which Gary studies, unabashed until he catches those lively, all-knowing grey eyes.

'Sorry, I thought the place was empty, like.' His heart is still thumping.

'It should have been, but I came back early. I never heard you come. I was out the back. Not to worry, *bach*. Come into the kitchen. Don't worry about your boots.' She walks in stiffly.

Gary follows her into the kitchen and back in time. There's a scrub-top table with pastry partly rolled on it, a settle and a dresser filled with blue, willow-patterned china, russet-coloured jugs, plates in inky blue, gold and white. The range is alight, with real coal, and a large black kettle hanging from an iron bracket in the flames. It's like an illustration from a children's story book.

'You still use the range to cook on?' asks Gary, taken aback.

'Nothing better. Your mum's got a 'lectric cooker, I suppose.'

'Gas.'

'Don't know how you can use them things. The food tastes like antiseptic. *Ych a fi.* Sit down, young man. What's your name?'

'Gary.'

'Sit down, Gary, and I'll make you some proper tea from a proper kettle.' She swings the now-steaming kettle across on the crane.

Gary sits obediently on the settle, watching all her movements. He feels very relaxed now, as if there's all the time in the world. He wants to know more about this old lady, but he's a bit shy to ask. She seems to sense this and anticipates his questions.

'I was born in this house. I've been back here more than fourteen years now. I nursed my sister 'til she died. My husband was a Greek, you know. I lived out there for thirty-five years.' She turns misty-eyed and wistful for a moment, her soul temporarily transported to a faraway land.

Gary doesn't know about Greece. Except that there's beaches there and discos and temples. And something they drink. He can't remember the name now.

'Ouzo. That's what my husband used to drink. He used to talk politics. He was a communist from after the war. The Greeks! She throws up her arms in despair. One minute you love them, next minute you hate them.'

Gary studies her determined features. He wonders if she and her husband used to quarrel.

'We 'ad some fights, him and me. Boy, we 'ad some fights.'
She chuckles to herself as she pours out the tea. 'We used
to throw plates and things at each-other. We made up after,
mind.' A mischievous grin spreads across her face. 'Breaking
plates was normal for them, you see. They used to do it by
purpose at weddings. I wouldn't. I always thought it was a
waste.' She puts the cup in front of Gary. 'Help yourself to
sugar now, go on.' She puts some Welsh cakes under his nose.
'Go on, take a couple. Don't be shy.'

Gary nibbles at a Welsh cake, thinking about this odd
faraway country with plates flying everywhere.

'It's the music and dancing I miss.' She closes her eyes and
Gary knows that she's hearing that far off music and dancing
to it. 'The *Panagia* was my favourite festival. There was a
dance where we all held hands and shuffled sideways to the
music in a big wide circle.' She describes it with a sweep of the
hand. 'The music is not like Welsh music. You don't snuggle
into it with tears in your eyes; it grabs you and lifts you up
and carries you along. It's always changing. Just that little bit.
There's no conductor. They seem to play as one.' She skips
and shuffles sideways across the kitchen, both hands linked to
imaginary dancers, being lifted along by inaudible music.

There's a loud knock on the door. They jump. The old lady
goes out of the room and makes her way down the passage.
Gary follows her and watches as she opens the front door.

'Mrs Annie Alexiou?' I'm Bryn Thomas from the
Environmental Health and Housing Department.'

'Come in, come in.'

'I understand that you've applied for a Renovation Grant ...'
He's a tallish man, with dark, curly hair and a moustache, a
little overweight, with a striped shirt and tie and a grey suit

creased at the back from sitting in the car. Even in that dark passageway, she reads him like a book. He finds the house distasteful, he thinks she's a decrepit old fool and he wants to get away as soon as possible. But she doesn't blame him for this. Nobody can help what they think, after all.

'Let me show you what's wrong,' she suggests. 'There's only a couple of things. There's a window that's rotten and the roof needs ...' She looks round, but he's no longer there. He's in the parlour, taking copious notes.

'But there's nothing wrong in there,' she protests, poking her head through the door. He ignores her until he's finished what he's writing, then looks up, a little condescendingly. 'We have to assess the condition of the property, to ascertain whether or not it is fit. We will, however, consider those items the owner brings to our attention.'

'Fit, how do you mean fit, *bach*?'

He smiles awkwardly. 'Fit for human habitation.'

'What? You're telling me that I live in a pigsty? I'll have you know that this place is cleaned from top to bottom young man, there's cheek!'

He raises a hand to stop her saying any more. 'I am not saying for a moment that your house is not well kept, Mrs Alexiou. On the contrary, it's spotless.' She relaxes her confrontational pose a little. He continues: 'I am merely saying that certain aspects of the fabric may not be up to modern fitness standards.'

'What fabric, the curtains?'

'No, the fabric of the building, the structure of the building.'

'Oh.'

We're in the kitchen now, and Mr Thomas is surprised to see the range still in use. He feels an overwhelming sense of shame and indignation that there are still people in Wales being forced to live in these conditions.

'We can give you a brand, spanking new kitchen: cooker, fridge, worktops, the lot. You won't have to cook on this lot ever again,' he says magnanimously, expecting the sun to come out all over her face.

'I've always cooked on the range, I'm not about to change now,' she says darkly. Mr Thomas says nothing. He asks to see the rest of the house. At the back is a small lean-to dairy and upstairs there are three bedrooms with boarded partitions partly in the slope of the roof, one tiny one in the middle, two large. Mr Thomas takes lots of notes. When they've been all round, he looks puzzled. 'There's no bathroom then?'

'The *tŷ bach* is out the back. At the bottom of the garden.'

'What about the bath?'

She looks irritated. She regards it as an affront to her dignity and privacy to be asked about her personal habits. He decides to deal with that one from the safety of his office, twenty miles away.

He shows himself to the door, clip pad in hand, a clip pad that leaves a trail of destruction wherever it goes. In just twenty minutes, that clip pad has done more damage to the old house than if someone had set off a grenade in the hall.

Gary is pedalling away furiously at an exercise bike. He's been through a punishing round of exercise training and this is the last item. He's been coming to the Sports Centre for three weeks now, at 7.30pm on Tuesdays, the same time that Sue does her keep fit session across the hall. He wants her to admire his rippling muscles, but she seems to be unaware of his presence.

But Sue's seen him alright. She thinks he's sweet: the way he throws furtive glances in her direction, with that hungry look. She stretches her left leg out luxuriously, in time with the music, and sees that flicker of a reaction on his face. When the session finishes, he will be having a cup of coffee in the hall, waiting for her to come out, hoping for a hello or a chat. She decides to sneak out the back. Chuckling to herself, she trots along the gravel path at the base of the building, sports bag in hand and comes to the front and looks in through the glass of the main entrance hall. There he is, sitting on one of the easy chairs, looking forlornly into the dregs of his coffee, wondering where she is. 'Oh! Bless him! The lost lamb.'

Does she want him? Or doesn't she? Does she? Doesn't she? She could almost toss a coin. He's a sensitive kid and she knows that with a bit of confidence, he could be amusing and good company. But there's a basic insecurity there, and she's not sure whether she wants to take that on board. He's changed a lot since she first saw him, filled out a little, doesn't look so gangly. And the odd, bleached hairstyle has gone; he's just got close-cropped hair. A bit of a hunk really.

Maybe someone will snap him up, and then she'll be sorry. She decides to keep him on the boil for a bit, until she makes up her mind about Brian. Anyway, she quite likes him like this, wanting her. It's quite flattering. Love him! She raps hard on the window. He turns round, sees her smiling and waving at him furiously behind the glass and almost chokes on his coffee. Giggling to herself, she runs to her car and speeds off.

Graham Parry has been doing plans for three years now. He worked for the council for a couple of years, learned how to draw, then started up on his own. He thought it would be lucrative, but he hadn't reckoned on overheads and the amount of actual productive hours he could do in a day. He ended up making, if anything, less than he did working for the council. Until the new grants came in, that is, and the council started paying big money in fees.

Mrs Alexiou's house is a typical grant job. Complete gut, floors up, new kitchen, raised ceilings, raised roof, new windows. It will come to maybe £90,000, a figure which will earn him a tidy percentage in fees, several times more than he would get if the council wasn't paying. It's a fairly simple job too, they're all much the same these old houses; you can guess a lot of the details.

There's something very grey about Graham, although he's only in his early thirties. There's a powdered, dusty look about him. He has a tired looking beard, a sort of greeny jumper of a non-descript colour and faded jeans. He sits next to Mrs Alexiou now at her kitchen table, methodically going through the plans. She looks drawn and apprehensive, the heavy lines on her face more taut than ever. But he doesn't see a vulnerable old lady and a vulnerable old house. The fat cheque is practically all that he sees. His civility is not calculated to the last dram, but there isn't much surplus.

She's giving him a hard time. Why did she listen to her son-in-law? It was his idea, not hers. She always had misgivings about it. She doesn't want to do the job anymore, she doesn't want her house wrecked.

Wrecked! thinks Graham. How do you explain to some people? She's going to get an almost brand new house. Anyway, it's a bit late now. The plans have been approved, and Davies Construction are starting in two weeks. She'll see sense, and when the job's finished, she'll thank them.

'Why do we have to raise these ceilings?' she protests.

'Because they're under eight feet,' Graham replies, smiling patiently.

'What difference does that make? I'm only five-foot two. At my age, I'm not going to grow any more, am I?'

'It's just the regulations.'

'Now let me get this straight.' She's got her reading glasses on, and she's on the ball. 'Because they want to raise these ground floor ceilings, all the upstairs walls will be gone, the roof will have to be made higher, the windows will have to be made higher. That means there will be nothing left.'

'But everything will be new. There's no need to worry. They'll pay for everything.'

'I don't want everything to be new. It won't be my house anymore.' There's a desperate childlike anxiety on her face. They're going to steal her life-blood. Now, at her age, they're going to pull the rug from under her, tear her home apart.

'Do they think about where I'm supposed to live when all this goes on? I only wanted a few repairs done,' she pleads, tears in her eyes.

'Have you got relatives?' asks Graham, wearing his mask of concern, glancing at his watch.

'No, I've decided,' she says stubbornly, 'I'm going to get a caravan in the yard. I'm going to stick here like glue. Otherwise, the next thing, the council are going to try and put me in a home. I'll come back here, and the door will be locked.'

'I don't think so,' says Graham. Again, that patronising smile.

'And what about these floors?' she says looking down at the quarry tiles. Why do you have to pull these floors up? '

'They're damp. These tiles are probably on earth.'

'They're dry as a bone. And if they're alright today, they'll be alright tomorrow. What's the difference? If you ask me, it's money down the drain. It's disgusting. Nothing left of this lovely old house but four walls. It's mad.'

Graham sighs.

Gary is rowing without enthusiasm. He's sat on a rather strange-looking machine with a white tubular structure and black padded seat. As he heaves the handle towards him, a screen in front shows a diagrammatic oarsman on a river and measures his performance. Not very good so far.

The trouble is that a certain person is missing from the keep-fit class. All this exercise has suddenly become less important. In fact, the strident voice of the keep-fit instructress across the hall is beginning to irritate him. He decides to call it a day.

As he takes his shower, Gary starts wondering. Maybe she's stopped coming because of him. The stalker! But she seemed friendly enough last week. Then he has a thought. What if she mentions casually to Brian that she sees him at exercise training every week? His eyes go into a fixed stare. He drops the bottle of shower gel onto his foot.

Awel Deg is being torn apart. Annie sits in a little caravan in the front yard, under the shade of the sycamore tree, looking anxiously out of the window at her dying home. It's out of her hands now. She can hear terrible banging and ripping noises emanating from inside. She can feel its pain. The front door opens at regular intervals and broken, battered bits of her life emerge and pass before her reddened eyes. All that effort, all that care, all that simple family history needlessly discarded and destroyed. And for what? Nobody seems able to give a reason.

They've set fire to the pile of timbers. They're burning it. She can't watch that. She suddenly feels sick and weak. She turns away, but the smell reaches her nostrils. The smell of pointless, swift, irretrievable destruction: two-hundred-year-old timbers that would last another two hundred years, painstakingly adzed and draw-knifed by a forgotten people with forgotten attitudes; old pit-sawn floorboards, hand-moulded partitions. It burns so easily. It doesn't fight back. It can't fight back.

There's a knock on the window. It's Gary. He's wearing a dust mask. His face and hair are powdered white. He removes the mask to reveal a clean oval of skin round his mouth. He looks a bit like a clown. She forces a smile and points towards the door.

'Are you alright?' asks Gary with genuine concern, stepping up into the caravan, looking self-consciously at his boots.

'Come in, *bach*, come in. Don't worry about your boots.' She scolds him for fussing. 'Let me make you some tea. I'm not very good with this gas.' She turns on the switch.

Gary leaps forward. 'Let me light it for you.'

'No, I can do it.' She frowns with determination as her gnarled, arthritic fingers struggle to light a match. 'Whump!' They both jump, then laugh together. She puts the kettle on the flames.

'Same as the range, really, only more excitable.'

She's reaching up into the cupboard now for some cups. Gary says: 'It's a pity what they're doing to your house. It was a nice old place. There'll be nothing left of it.' She stiffens, hand on the cupboard knob with her back to Gary. She starts shaking. Gary looks concerned. Maybe she's having some kind of fit. Should he call a doctor?

'Mrs Alexiou, are you alright?' He leans forward, but she's got her head almost touching the cupboard door. It's hard to see her face. Then he sees, and he recoils back. She's sobbing, sobbing her heart out, her little body in spasms.

Gary feels very awkward and inadequate. What's he supposed to do? He touches her shoulder, very gently. 'Mrs ...' he doesn't know what to say. Maybe he should say, 'It's alright', but obviously it isn't. Or he could say, 'Come on now, Mrs Alexiou,' but there's enough people pushing her around already.

She stops shaking and begins to pull herself together. She goes to her handbag, pulls out a lace hanky, and begins to dry her eyes. 'I'm sorry my love, I shouldn't have done that to you.'

'No, it's alright, there's no ... you can ...'

'There's an old softee I am. All over a silly old house. Fancy crying over a house, stupid old bag.' Gary wants to say, 'No, you're not,' but he's tongue-tied. He hopes she doesn't think he agrees.

They're sat now, at a Formica-topped table, drinking their tea, Mrs Alexiou with her back to the window which faces the house. She's perked up a little, putting on a brave face. They say nothing for a minute, then Gary plucks up courage and asks how she met her husband.

She sighs, a long sigh which transports her back through the years. 'I met him in London, love.'

'You lived up there?'

'No, we had relatives up that way. When the war was on, they used to come down and stay, for a rest from the bombing. They looked so pale and tense, poor loves, it took ages to relax them; and of course, my mother used to stuff them with food.

The rations didn't affect us much. We could get most things. By the time they went back, they were all rosy-cheeked and healthy-looking. I tell you what I remembered about them: whenever we decided to do anything, they wanted to do it there and then; not in a day or two, or even in ten minutes, now, straight away. I suppose to them there might not be a tomorrow.

Gary studies her face. She's looking pale and tense too. Not the button-eyed Mrs Alexiou she was when he first called at the house.

'We used to offer to come and see them in London, but they always said no. It was silly to go and risk our lives too, they said, when we didn't have to. But when the war ended, we did go up. It was an awful sad sight to see whole streets just flattened to the ground. What a mess. I'll never forget that first trip into London. We all felt so guilty that we had been safe when they were going through hell. And now they're going to do the same thing here.' She laughs a cynical laugh. 'Who would believe, this house was safe in the war and now in peacetime it isn't. '

She looks at Gary. 'Sorry love, I haven't answered your question.' Gary shrugs, an easy-going shrug. He could listen to Mrs Alexiou for days.

'I met my husband on that first trip. He was a friend of my cousin. I couldn't believe all the hand movements. I hadn't seen anything like it before. He was so alive. Everyone else looked dead and flat to compare with him.

'Did you get married in Greece?' Gary can imagine a mad wedding with everyone having to duck because of flying plates.

'No, we got married down here, then went out to Iannis' island and he opened a small *taverna*.'

'Taverna?'

'A bar, love, like a pub.'

'Oh.'

'My dad said, "Mark my words, she'll return in a month with her tail between her legs." But I didn't. It was primitive, mind, but that didn't bother me. I was young and adaptable.'

'I expect it was hot, was it?'

She hands him a bit of currant cake on an old willow-patterned plate. 'Very hot on days when there was no breeze. It was refreshing to go into the sea. I learnt to swim, but I wasn't much cop. My husband could swim like a fish. He used to go out most mornings to fish for octopus. They used to have it with their ouzo, barbecued octopus legs chopped up like a banana. And they cooked it other ways.'

'Gary grimaces. Wouldn't it tangle up the line?'

'What line, *bach*?'

'The fishing line.'

She smiles. 'No, they didn't fish with a rod. They used to swim out, go underwater and catch them with their bare hands.'

Gary has visions of Mr Alexiou grappling with a giant octopus. Every time he hacks off a leg, another one gets a grip on him. It seems like a lot of effort, just for a snack with your ouzo. 'How big were they?'

'About the size of your fist, with eight long tentacles coming off it.'

'Oh.'

'That's how he met his end, doing that, bless him.'

Gary looks embarrassed. 'It's alright, you don't have to …'

'Don't worry my love, it's a long time ago now. Though it seems like yesterday to me.'

Gary looks thoughtfully into his tea, not daring to look up in case Mrs Alexiou once again goes into floods of tears.

'I knew there was something wrong. Crowds of people were gathered on the beach and they all looked dark and brooding. And when I went down, they made way for me. There was a tiny island, more like a lump of rock really, off the headland. A couple of swimmers were bringing something in from there. I knew it had to be him, but you hope, don't you, that you're wrong. When they brought him to the shore, he was face down in the water, and I remember thinking, "Maybe any second now, he'll turn over and laugh at me."'

Gary is concentrating on a tiny speck of dirt on the side of his cup.

'I'll never forget seeing those people all lined up on the beach. They didn't move. They were absolutely still, like statues. My husband had dived or something and hit his head on a rock. Nobody knew for sure and they didn't dwell on it. He was dead, and that was that.'

There's a loud crash outside. Brian has just thrown a door onto the blazing pile. He's looking round now, wondering where Gary is. 'I'd better go, Gary frowns, otherwise they'll murder me.'

Sue floats down the passageway towards the entrance hall of the Sports Centre where Gary is sitting as usual. She's wearing tight jeans and a white woolly jumper pulled right down over her legs. She's just had a shower and her face is red and shining. Her hair is still damp and she keeps raising it with her hands and shaking her head violently from side to side to help dry it.

'Hi Gary, fancy some coffee? I'm thirsty as hell.' A breeze of perfume hits him.

'Yes, I'll get it,' he says in one short exhalation. He swims his way towards the vending machine. Sue settles herself on the sofa and watches, bemused as he fumbles in his wallet for the money. When he's put the money in, he'll realise that he doesn't know how she likes her coffee.

'Oh, um, how d'you like your coffee?' he asks, wandering back towards where she's sat. He's come all over in a sweat.

'Black no sugar.'

He finally struggles back with the coffees and sits a good foot away from Sue on the sofa. She doesn't rush to drink her coffee, for someone who's so thirsty.

'Bit of a star on the exercise machine, eh Gary?' she says. 'You must be pretty fit doing that night after night.'

'No, um, well it helps with work like, you can get through the day better if you're fit,' he mumbles. He doesn't say this is the only night he's here.

'Have you injured your leg? It looked a bit twisted when I saw you walking just now.'

He gives a kind of hunted look. 'I broke it when I was a kid. It didn't set very well.'

'How?'

'I think I fell downstairs, I don't remember.' In fact, his mother had gone out with a boyfriend, leaving him alone in the house. He had a nightmare and, half-asleep, blundering down the stairs in search of her, he fell to the bottom and broke his leg. He lay there in agony for seven hours until she returned. It was another hour before he reached the hospital and it had to be re-set.

They chat for a while, but Sue is not happy. There's something about the look on his face that she can't put her finger on. It's as if he's pulling at her. She gulps down her coffee and makes her excuses rather hurriedly. She's decided to go and see Brian, to wipe away the cobwebs. That's the good thing about men, you can turn them on like a tap, whenever you want.

She gets into the car and she's about to start the engine when she sees a caterpillar slowly crawling up the windscreen. Irritably, she reaches for the windscreen wiper switch, but stops herself in time and finds a piece of paper on the passenger seat instead. Then, getting out of the car, she very gently eases the caterpillar onto the paper and puts it safely under a nearby bush.

Brian and Gary sit on the roof of Awel Deg, lobbing slates into a skip below. Small clouds of grey dust and dead cluster flies follow them down. Gary marvels at these old-fashioned slates that he has never seen before. Instead of being nailed, there are pegs tightly fitted into holes drilled in the slates, which hook onto thin laths running between the rafters. The top corners have been rounded and as he removes them, he imagines them as little grey shirts on a washing line. He wonders who put them there and how long ago.

Gary feels as if he has blood on his hands, doing this work. He's not sure that he likes Brian anymore. Everything he does and says seems to be destructive. He takes pleasure now in throwing these hand-crafted slates and smashing them to bits in the skip below. Even when he is building, not demolishing, it's a destructive process for Brian. He tears and rips the saw through the wood, then impales it with nails and beats it into submission. You won't see him using a hand plane either: it's too close for comfort – too much shared with the wood. No, chew it up with an electric planer. It's quicker. That's Brian.

He gets to wondering how he treats Sue. Maybe he treats her the same. He couldn't bear that.

It's a beautiful clear April morning and from his vantage point on the roof, Gary can see for miles around. To his left, the land dips down steeply into a secluded valley, a little green patch of heaven on earth, with a tiny grey church at its base. He could reach out and play dominoes with the gravestones. Over the rise is the sea, a broad stretch of pastel blue, all fluffed up with the sky so you can't see the join. A bright red fishing boat churns its way slowly north, making the only waves that morning. Ahead and to his right, a network of bluey-green fields strung haphazardly together with stone hedges gradually gives way in the distance to a scrubland of heather and gorse. In the far distance, the faint outlines of the mountains of Snowdonia are etched against the skyline. But for the ivory-coloured sheep grazing in the foreground with their new-born lambs and the pendulum motion of the gulls in the sky, everything might have frozen into a still picture.

Gary feels that a part of him wants to break free, float out and dissolve into that landscape. He gets embarrassed by feelings like this. Sometimes he gets this fear, that he may be going mad. Who else would think such daft things?

The day passes like a waking dream, constantly interrupted by the smashing of slates and groans of protest as rafter after rafter is torn away from its supporting purlins and hurled into the yard below. Gary watches from the ridge as the van finally bounces down the drive. Through the back windows, he glimpses its tired human cargo being tossed this way and that before it heads off down the road. Gary is borrowing the pickup tonight, to fetch some furniture for his mother. Mrs Alexiou has been limewashing the yard walls, numb now to the chaos and destruction around her. Gary gets down from the roof, in no hurry to leave,

'That's funny paint. It goes all grey at first, then it dries very white,' he observes, with that typically curious look on his face.

'It's whitewash,' says Mrs Alexiou. 'It's made from this lime you get in bags. It's not much good. It flakes off.' She slops some more on the wall resignedly with a big floppy brush. 'I remember they used to throw lumps into an old tank full of water. It used to fizz like the devil and you couldn't touch the side of the tank for the heat. That stuff used to stick, mind. When I was a child, we used to lime the house a different colour every year. My mother mixed the lime and put powders in. If the colour went wrong, she was so upset, she used to cry.'

'Cry?'

'I know, it's difficult to believe, but she was so proud of the way the house looked.' She glances at Gary, suddenly spots something, and stares intently into his eyes. 'There's a different look with you. Now then, what is it, there's a girl, isn't there?'

Gary looks awkward, 'Well not exactly, I mean ...'

'There you are,' says Mrs Alexiou triumphantly, 'I'm good like that, I can tell things by just looking.'

'You can't read people's minds?' asks Gary worriedly. A shiver goes down his spine.

'I can't tell exactly what people are thinking, but I can tell what they are feeling. You feel a lot for this girl, but I don't think she's right for you. Never mind, you're young enough to find out the hard way. Are you courting?'

'Courting? What's that?'

'Let me see, what is it you young people say, are you going out with her?'

'Well, um, no. She's my partner's girlfriend.'

'Oh dear, well you'll have to decide what's more important I suppose.'

The rugby field at Tairffynnon is cut into a slope, forming banks on three sides. In bad weather, they're a muddy quagmire with kids running and sliding up and down them. But on a good day like today, they form excellent tiered seating for spectators. On the fourth side, the ground falls down to the road and opposite is a row of former council houses. They used to be dull grey, but recently they've come out in a variety of queasy colours. If you look carefully into the upstairs windows, you'll see people watching the game intently from the comfort of their homes. There's a crowd of supporters shouting for Tairffynnon. 'COME ON FFYNNON! COME ON, FFYNNON!' Time is running out and they need another try. Gary climbs up the bank towards them.

Sue is on top of the bank, a little apart from the main group of spectators. Brian is in the team and she's jumping up and down excitedly, cheering them on. Gary comes up behind her, his heart thumping. 'Hi Sue!' She whirls round, says hello rather irritably and turns back to the game. What's he doing here? She frowns to herself.

Gary's standing next to her now. 'Exciting game?' he asks, a little unnecessarily, hands in pockets.

'Yeah.'

They can see Gwyn out in midfield. He ploughs on with the ball at walking pace and two opposition forwards hanging off him like parasites, until another has the sense to go for his legs and he comes down like an old oak tree.

'Are we winning?'

'Not yet.' The opposition winger comes rocketing past with the ball, just inside the touchline below them and is looking dangerous, but Brian comes across diagonally with a perfect tackle and they both slide into touch. As he gets to his feet, Brian catches a glimpse of Gary and Sue standing together. A tiny cloud comes over his face, but it disperses when they both cheer and clap him together.

'I wanted to ask you a question,' says Gary.

'Oh yeah,' says Sue. She's got a fair idea what.

'There's a good film on at The Lantern on Sunday, and I wondered if ...'

At first she's got this urge to tell him to piss off, but when she sees the look on his face, she relaxes into a warm smile. 'Gary, that's very sweet of you, but me and Brian are going steady.' She wants to say 'Maybe one day,' or something like that, but it wouldn't be fair to give him hope. Instead she says, 'You're a nice kid, Gary, there's plenty of more attractive girls than me around.'

'That's not true,' he says defiantly. 'That's a load of rubbish.'

'That's nice of you to say so. Are we still friends?'

He nods.

Gary wends his way back into the centre of town, body hunched forward, looking forlorn. As he nears the end of the street, there's a massive cheer and he turns round briefly. Tairffynnon have scored the winning try.

Something is wrong with Mrs Alexiou. It's the middle of the day and she's lying in bed. The back bedroom in her caravan is almost all bed, so it's difficult to get near to her. She's looking very grey, wheezing a lot and she's all red round the eyes. A tiny wrinkled white foot sticks out from under the blanket at the bottom of the bed.

'Are you alright, Mrs Alexiou?'

'Is that you Gary?' She tries to pull herself up but goes into a fit of coughing.

'Don't get up. Can I get you anything? Can I make you a cup of tea? Are you hungry?'

She shakes her head. 'If you could get me a big jug-full of water, *bach*, I'll be fine. Bless you.'

When Gary brings the water, he has to squeeze between the bed and the wall to get to her bedside table. As soon as he puts down the jug and glass, an arm comes across and grips his wrist like a clamp.

'Promise me something,' she pleads, willing him with her eyes.

'Yes ...'

'Promise you won't get a doctor. I don't want a doctor. They'll take me away. I want to stay here.' Gary looks worried. He's never been given this kind of responsibility before. What should he do? Should he humour her, then sneak off and get a doctor? He looks at her again. The eyes are no longer pleading. They're reprimanding him for his wayward thoughts, willing him to do as he asks.

'Alright, he says quietly. 'I won't. But someone has to look after you.'

'There's no need.'

'Haven't you got relatives?'

'No!' She's looking alarmed now. 'You mustn't tell anyone. Nobody must know.'

'I won't. I promise,' he says resignedly. That seems to satisfy her. She relaxes her grip on his wrist. A sort of peace comes over her. She studies Gary's face carefully. For a minute, she's the old Mrs Alexiou, the one he first met.

'So you asked her out and she said no?'

Gary nods.

'Never mind, there are plenty more fish in the ocean.'

'She seemed to like me. I don't understand.'

'Maybe you're too serious about her. She's young. She just wants to enjoy herself. Lighten up a bit and you'll be fighting off the women.'

The girl at the music counter doesn't respond for a second. It's a busy Saturday morning and she looks harassed. 'Greek music?' she asks loudly. Gary looks around furtively, in case anyone is listening. Why does she have to shout? 'Oh, hang on, wait a second now, I've seen something before ...' She reaches below the counter and eventually straightens up holding a single tape in her hand. 'Greek Island Songs.' She passes the tape over to Gary. All the songs are listed in funny writing. This must be the genuine article.

'How much?'

It's quite smelly in Mrs Alexiou's caravan when Gary returns that afternoon. He opens one of the windows. Mrs Alexiou is lying almost motionless and looking very grey. The jug of water from the day before has been knocked over and there's a damp stain on the floor. Odd gargling noises are coming from deep down in her chest; a sort of snoring sound. Suddenly feeling a bit stupid, Gary puts the tape recorder on the bottom of the bed and wonders whether to turn it on or not.

'Mrs Alexiou?' She doesn't respond, but there's a faint smile on her face. Annie Evans is a million miles away, running full pelt downhill through a summery meadow in her favourite dress. She opens her arms out wide just in case she finds that she can fly. Down below, the men in their waistcoats are scything all in a line. She can smell the freshly-cut hay and hear them conversing and laughing as they work.

She's in the kitchen at home now, staring intently at her father. He's sat on a stool by the range, looking into the flames, the tiredness written all over his face. She can smell the earth and sweat on him and the acrid smoke from his pipe. He coughs violently and spits into the fire. It hisses angrily back at him. In the back room, the *llaethdy*, she can hear a clap-clap sound as her mother smacks a pat of butter into shape. Her brother is teasing her, trying to push her off the chair.

It's gone all bright now. Bright bright. She's looking towards the sun, but a figure slowly materialises in front of her. It's Iannis. They're in his taverna, surrounded by familiar faces. She can hear the haunting island music. It's so near and so clear. A song she hasn't heard before. It's beautiful.

Mrs Alexiou starts coughing, a desperate, grasping, fighting, snatching kind of cough. Then she goes still, frozen. Gary knows that she has died. He turns the tape recorder off. He's very shaken. For a few minutes, he panics. Should he call the doctor? Should he call the ambulance? But he knows, he has to leave. He hasn't been here. He picks up the tape recorder, shuts the caravan window and goes out quietly through the door. As he goes out, he sees a photo on the shelf he hasn't noticed before. The Alexiou newlyweds. He realises that he's attracted to the young Annie in the photo. It's quite a shock. He stumbles toward the caravan door.

Outside, the fresh April air is a relief. Gary's glad to be alive. He feels a little taller as he walks to his car, a bit like he felt walking through town in his first pair of boots on his first day at work.

Awel Deg has been reduced to four stone walls up to first floor level. The upper walls were demolished because of the odd bulge here and there. Mrs Alexiou's son-in-law will be happy with his new house: spar dash, plastic windows, breakfast bar, corner bath, gold taps, the lot.

5

PIPE DREAM

A brightly-painted old fishing boat braves the channel between Tairffynnon harbour and Ynys y Ddraig, Dragon's Island, bobbing and weaving its way through the choppy waters. Now and again, the bow nose-dives into the crest of a wave, sending a cold, salty spray past the wheelhouse into the open deck behind. Normally, the passengers would be a stoically cheerful collection of day trippers and twitchers. But today's party is more serious and thoughtful. There's an agenda here. There's confrontation in the air.

They've divided themselves into two camps. The Planning Committee sits in a row along the port side benching, trying to maintain its corporate dignity, almost pretending it is not on a boat, but in the council chamber. Opposite, on the starboard side, is a predominantly young, informally-dressed group, who converse with each-other earnestly in subdued tones.

A fin appears above water off the port side, quite close to the boat. 'Shark!' shouts one of the councillors.

'Don't be daft, Dai, it's a dolphin,' says a female colleague.

'Dolphin!' shouts one of the starboard side group, and as one, they rush across to the port side as the dolphin performs a series of leaps and dives. The boat tips to one side alarmingly.

'Sit down!' comes an angry roar from the wheelhouse and they return meekly to their places just as a speedboat roars past on their side, competing with the dolphin for attention. Jim and Graham Parry sit nervously at the back. Their driver, Ian Bartlett, rich businessman, has defiant features: fair, straggly hair blowing back in the wind, jaw thrust stubbornly forward. He waves cheekily at the occupants of the fishing boat as if this is all a wheeze for him.

Sat next to him is wife number three, her face partly hidden by a red scarf. She glances across briefly, then presents them with her profile once more. What's she thinking as she stares straight ahead into the surf? She's thinking about a home, a base, a garden; a place to decorate, to furnish, to entertain people in; a bit of stability. But on an island?

The boat hugs the dark, brooding cliff face as it rounds the northern end of the island. Rows of guillemots, live piano keys, jostle for position on a high ledge above. The rocks are streaked all over with guano. The gulls circle overhead, announcing the arrival of intruders. Presently, the bow heads towards a narrow gap between the cliffs and a tall, solitary lump of rock, which broke away from the land aeons ago and now forms the entrance to a natural harbour. From a distance, it looks like an animal, some kind of spiky animal, a dinosaur maybe.

'Stay in your places now!' comes a reprimanding voice from the wheelhouse as the engine slows down and they chug into a narrow inlet with vertical cliffs on three sides. The engine noise rattles about in the confined space. The boat immediately stops rolling and glides through calm water, bringing relief to several faces. Ahead of them, a wooden jetty and a corrugated iron shed have been built off a stony beach, the posts worn and pitted by the tides. The boat pulls in next to Ian's speedboat and the passengers disembark.

Ian Bartlet stands just off the jetty and shouts cheerfully to his guests: 'This way, ladies and gentlemen!' They follow him, but he soon disappears out of sight along a lane that heads inland from the harbour, passing a complex of red-painted tin sheds. Familiar smells and lowing cattle tell us that we have sailed right into a farm. Ian's farm is a little bizarre, but it works. The cattle are milked down at the harbour and the milk is pumped into a milk-tank on board a boat. The boat crosses the half-mile to the mainland to be met by the road tanker. Obviously, you need someone to be living on the spot with all that calving, sick cattle, the danger of being cut off by storms and so on, so Ian has applied for planning permission to build an agricultural dwelling. Simple.

Ian's party are now standing on the site for the new house. It's on the west side of a valley, 400 yards from the harbour, with a small stream in front and scrub as a backdrop. Directly behind, beyond the scrub, is a superb sandy beach at the bottom of the cliffs. While the others chat and await the arrival of the Planning Committee, Ian goes through long-terms plans in his head. He's going to build another jetty down on that beach, where guests can arrive and moor their expensive boats. After all, he doesn't want them coming up through a farmyard. At the back of the beach, a pair of wrought iron lockable gates in the cliff face will guard the approach: a tunnel, like a smugglers' cave, carved into the rock, with steps leading up to the house.

As his guests emerge, blinking from the dim light of the tunnel, they'll enter a beautiful walled garden with climbing plants, a fountain and formal shrubbery. At this point, they'll be offered a refreshing drink (Pimms? G and T, ice-cold lager?) by a servant, who will take their cases up a half-flight to the first floor while they descend into the living area. Here, a huge, glazed window will reveal the island in all its glory. In the foreground will be a large, landscaped garden with the existing stream skilfully used to create a whole series of ponds ...

'Here they come!' Graham shouts. They can see heads now, bobbing up and down in the lower field, the bodies concealed by a hump in the ground. Gradually, the figures grow from the neck downward as they climb the rise. It's like a battalion approaching. 'Think small,' Ian tells himself, as they gather round him. 'No harbours, no tunnels in the rock, just a simple agricultural dwelling for the farm manager.' The inquisitive cattle, as if on cue, have come to join the throng and the meeting opens to the accompaniment of ripping grass and swishing tails.

'... the application is for an agricultural dwelling ... we have established that there is a valid need for a dwelling on the site ... there have been a number of objections on environmental grounds ...' The planning chief reads out some letters on recycled paper. A cow bellows and much of the content is lost on the breeze.

The portly man in the buff mack has now taken centre stage. He's Tom Jones (Councillor Jones to you), stomach puffed out like a robin in cold weather. Very important, Mr Jones. He's allowed himself to be harnessed by the conservationists. Less to do with deep-felt beliefs we suspect, than because Ian failed to come and crawl to him about the application.

'We are very concerned,' he begins. 'What will become of the birds? This island belongs to nature ...' with a dramatic sweep of the hand. 'Human beings have no place here.' General nods from the conservationists.

'My God,' mutters Councillor Warner, 'Tom's gone green.'

'He didn't look too good on the boat,' observes Councillor Rees, turning his head so as not to be overheard.

'… cormorant, gannet, razorbills, guillemots, to name but a few. I wonder,' continues Tom. 'Will they want to stay with human beings on the island? They'll all fly somewhere else.'

'I wish *he* would,' mutters Councillor Warner.

Councillor Jones drones on and a girl in a yellow waterproof top gets increasingly edgy. At last, she can no longer contain herself. 'It's all a front,' she shouts,' he just wants a des-res to show off to his rich friends. He …'

'Quiet!' The chairman of the Planning Committee silences her with a downward wave of the hand. This is a committee meeting, not a free-for-all.'

But Ian rather likes this girl. She's genuine and she's got spirit; yet to be bogged down by the protocol and barter and compromise of local politics. 'Let her speak,' he urges.

The chairman asks her name.

'Sarah Bowden.'

He gestures for her to continue.

'He buys an island, turns it into a farm, just so he can build a posh house here.' She points an accusing finger at Ian. 'Next thing we'll have big yachts mooring here. Jetskis, microlights, helicopters coming back and fore. Private plane, airstrip. Clay pigeon shoots. It'll be a rich man's playground; the farm will be forgotten about.'

Conservationist heads are nodding vigorously. Ian smiles good-naturedly. Not even a scratch on that rhinoceros hide.

'He's putting the wool on our eyes,' says Councillor Jones,

slaughtering his metaphors. 'This is just the tip of the icing.'

'Perhaps Mr Bartlet can tell us,' Sarah continues, 'whether he really cares about the birds.'

'Of course I care about the birds,' says Ian, smiling benignly, 'we get along just fine.' He pauses to brush a forelock back over this head. 'They don't bother me and I don't bother them. I don't stalk them and watch them through binoculars all day.' He imitates binoculars with his forefingers and thumbs. 'I don't ring them, study their offspring, pester them, so-called monitoring their progress. I leave them to get on with their lives. They leave me to get on with mine.'

'Oh very noble!' she declares sarcastically. 'That's stupid and you know it. How can they lead normal lives if the island becomes your playground? They'll feel threatened and leave.'

Unruffled, Ian smiles charmingly, the tap of sincerity full on. 'I'm simply applying for an agricultural dwelling, so that the farm can be managed properly.' He stands, arms wide, an open-defences pose. 'If cattle are suffering and dying because nobody is here to help them, is that what you want? All this playground bit is nonsense. Take a look at the application.' He holds out a sheet of paper, which flaps in the breeze. 'Does it say anything here about a theme park?'

'This is the thin end of the wedge,' mutters one of the conservationists. Jim and Graham look at the ground.

'Well, thank you for your comments,' says the committee chairman abruptly and without a further word, the councillors turn their hindquarters towards the onlookers and form a standing circle to discuss the application in subdued tones. Then, all at once, the huddle unfolds like the petals of a bedraggled flower. Within minutes, the backs of those same heads can be seen bobbing up and down in the distance. Before long, only Jim, Graham and the Bartlets are left, slightly dazed, not by the intensity, but by the brevity of it all.

'Well,' says Jim, to no one in particular, 'what do you think?'

'No probs,' says Ian with a grin.

Fay Bartlet looks down through the valley, past the harbour, across a stretch of sea, until her eye finally rests on the only thin strip of mainland that is visible in the distance.

It's a slightly misty morning on Ynys y Ddraig and the air is quite still. Only the distant machine-gun fire of magpies breaks the silence. The mist slowly clears from the glistening landscape like tissue-paper being lifted to reveal a precious jewel. A blue sky is beginning to break through and although it's only 8.30am, Jim can already feel the warmth of the sun on his face. It's going to be a scorcher.

But all is far from well. He frowns as he surveys the patchwork of concrete floor slabs spread out in a maze below him, the beginnings of Ian Bartlet's house. By the end of the previous day, large areas of blockwork had been rebuilt, and Brian and Gary had reconstructed the shuttering, plywood moulding for some of the concrete pillars and ground-beams. Now every wall has been violently pushed over for the second time and the shuttering has been torn apart, half-splintered ply with protruding nails scattered everywhere.

As he surveys the damage, he spots movement in the distance, and a prickly fear overtakes him. Ghostly figures begin to materialise out of the mist, which still envelops the lower part of the valley and the harbour. First one, then three, four, six figures approaching. If they're out to get him, he doesn't stand a chance. No point in running. But the foremost figure looks familiar and as it draws near, he can see it's Gwyn, then Gary and Brian behind, with John, Byron and Oar taking up the rear. As they take in the scene of destruction, a repeat of the previous morning, the men don't utter a word. They pore over the site, still holding their haversacks, silent figures in a waking dream.

Two things are going through Jim's mind. Who are the culprits, and will they strike again? He's not sure what to do and Ian can't be contacted. He doubts that Ian would want to inform the police and possibly end up with the press being involved. Better to try and find the culprits themselves first. But when will they strike next? Tomorrow? In a week's time? He figures that it's easier and quieter to demolish low walls recently put up, especially when the mortar is wet, than a half-built house. But with their victims on the alert, would they dare do it again?

'I'm coming here tonight,' growls Gwyn, 'and when I catch who's doing this, I'll use their heads to break blocks with.'

'Me too,' says Brian.

'I've got a good idea who it is,' says Jim. 'They were at the planning meeting. They don't want anyone living here because of the wildlife. And guess who their leader is?'

Blank faces.

'Sarah Bowden. She's back from college and making a nuisance of herself already.'

They look stunned. It's the one in the photo at the Bowden house. Suddenly, everyone wants to come.

'I think we've got a choice,' says John quietly, so that they have to strain to hear. 'Either we guard the site with bright lights and a video camera every night until the building is up, or we hide and pretend it's not guarded and catch them red-handed.'

'But they're going to expect us to be lying in wait tonight,' says Jim.

General agreement.

'So we do both.'

'Both?'

'We light up the site, with a hidden video, and put a guard on.'

'Yeah?'

'But we make sure the guard is crap, don't we?'

'How?'

'We give him a bottle of whisky to drink, which isn't whisky and he pretends to get as pissed as a pick and go to sleep. But they don't know there's others hiding in the scrub. So when they see he's asleep, they move in. Then we move in, and all but the last bit is on video.' He smacks the palm of his left hand with his right fist to illustrate his point.

'The Bowden woman is mine,' says Brian, with a salacious look. Instantly, Gary is worried for her.

'You'll have to go home,' says Jim, 'in the fishing boat as usual. Make plenty of noise, so anyone watching will know you're leaving. Then somehow, we'll have to secretly get you all back again. I'll be the guard. I'll come in the speedboat. It doesn't matter if they see me. They could be watching here, or on the mainland. He scratches his mop of black hair for a moment, then suddenly, he's got the answer. 'The bulk tank! You can come inside the bulk tank! In the bulk tank boat with the cowman.'

'*Ych a fi*,' Brian retorts, 'there'll be milk left in it.'

'No, it gets cleaned in the harbour on the mainland. The

boat comes right into one of the sheds here. You can hang about in the shed until dusk, then sneak up here through the scrub. That's it then: Gwyn, Brian and Byron. '

'What about me then?' Gary bleats.

'That's good of you to offer, Gary,' says Jim, 'but I don't think we're dealing with an army and three in the bulk tank will already be crowded.'

'He won't shut us in there?' asks Byron, claustrophobia already coming on.

'No need, the lid can be left off, or loose. It's supposed to be empty.

'That afternoon, as the boys battle on with re-building yet again, Jim returns with lighting, a generator and a video camera, which they attach, well-hidden, to one of the low trees in the scrub behind. By the end of the day, all the walls and shuttering are much as they were before being vandalised the previous night.

Brian and Gary are sat on the quay now, legs dangling over the sides. It's the end of the day and they've taken to bringing a few tins of beer each to swill down as they await the boat to take them back to the mainland. The others haven't come down yet.

'Here she comes!' The boat always appears quite suddenly from behind the headland. They catch sight and sound of it at the same time. It reaches the harbour in minutes, and, engine still running, hovers by the quayside. Seeing the others aren't down yet, Harry cuts out the engine and gets out his pipe.

Harry Popeye, as they call him, has been on boats all his life. Once upon a time, just fishing kept him and his family alive, but now he relies more and more heavily on boat trips. He's quite agile for his years and surprisingly slim. But if you've got a good nose, you can tell that while the salt is preserving his exterior, the alcohol is pickling his interior. He can't swim, and nearly lost his life once when he fell overboard after one drink too many. Luckily, there was a length of rope trailing off the back, which by some miracle he managed to grab onto. The boat did one full wide circle unmanned before he finally managed to haul himself on board again.

The little girls swarm round him like flies when he repairs his nets on the quayside at Tairffynnon. 'Come on, Harry, do your Popeye face. Oh come onnn. Oh pleeeeease!'

'Go away now, I'm busy.'

'Oh come onnn!' They flap up and down like chickens trying to fly. 'We'll leave you alone if you do it. Just once. Pleeease!

Beaten, Harry makes his face go all rubbery and pushes his pipe deep into a mouth that's been reduced to just a hole in the skin. They scream with delight, jumping up and down, nearly wetting themselves.

'Oooh, do it again, pleeease!'

Harry is lighting his pipe now, waiting for the others to come. 'I'm surprised you boys are building here,' he says, watching his smoke slowly drift across the harbour.

'Why?' asks Brian, half-interested, leaning against the side of the boat, hands in pockets.

'What with the legend and all.'

Brian looks away in disgust, but Gary, depressed about missing all the action that evening, perks up and asks, 'What legend?'

'The legend of the dragon.'

'I know Ynys y Ddraig means dragon's island,' says Gary, 'but I haven't heard no legend.'

'There was a dragon living here once,' Harry begins, with a glint in his eye, 'maybe there still is.' Brian raises his eyes to heaven, moves away a bit, nearly out of earshot and sits down again, his back half-turned.

'I've heard funny noises coming from the island at night, that's for definite,' Harry continues.

Gary shivers. 'Tell us about the legend.'

'This dragon wasn't like a normal dragon, he was dead easy-going like, he didn't hurt nobody. Even when the settlers came. '

'Settlers?'

'Aye. There were three brothers on the mainland, each with little kingdoms, but two picked on the one, understand me, so he came out here with his followers and settled on the island. He was more worried about his brothers than some tame dragon.'

'It would be a safe place, I suppose,' says Gary, thinking about all the high cliffs.

'There you are. Anyhow the dragon treated them tidy. No bother at all.'

'Something went wrong,' mutters Brian over his shoulder, 'it always does, otherwise there wouldn't be a legend, and we wouldn't have to listen to this bloody crap.'

Harry smiles, unruffled, draws at his pipe until the tobacco crackles, then bangs the bowl against the side of the boat. The contents hiss as they hit the water. 'Yeah, there was a smart-arse in the camp,' half-looking at Brian, 'decided he wanted to make a name for himself, see.'

'Doing what?' asks Gary.

'Killing a dragon. Killing a dragon would be like … winning an Olympic medal in them days. Trouble was, the dragon had done nothing wrong. He was tame. No bother. So what did he do? He framed the dragon for something he didn't do. One night, when he was out on guard, they had a herd of goats penned up. He went in and killed three goats, leaving a few bits behind like a head or a foot. He dropped the dead goats down a hole in the rocks. Then, clever bugger, he'd carved this dragon's foot out of wood and pushed it in the mud to look like footprints.' He pauses to refill his pipe, then looks up to see the rest of Jim's boys approaching. 'Then he got a torch and burnt the ground and some of his own clothes with it.'

'With a torch?' Gary looks puzzled.

'The torches in them days were made of burning fat.'

'Oh yeah, I've seen them in films.'

'So what does he do then, he rushes into the camp, screaming blue murder, saying that the dragon has attacked, nearly killed him, breathing fire everywhere, and made off with three goats. The next morning, they sent off a kind of posse, and our friend knew the cave where the dragon lived, and also knew what nobody else knew, that he always slept mornings.'

Jim's boys are leaping onto the boat now.

'What's he talking about?' asks John.

'A dragon,' Brian replies, 'and it doesn't half drag on.'

'So what happened,' asks Gary urgently, afraid he's going to miss the rest of the story.

'Our "hero" got the rest of the posse to stand with boulders on the cliffs above the cave opening to throw down at the dragon in case of trouble. Convenient see, they couldn't watch. Then, looking very brave, he went into the cave alone with his spear to kill the dragon. Sure enough, the dragon was asleep, but there was something he didn't count on.'

'The dragon slept with one eye open,' suggests Brian with a sigh.

'There you are, he's right. Our hero was burnt to a crisp before he could lift the spear even. He looked like a piece of bacon you'd forgotten under the grill. Then the dragon flew out of the cave and burnt the whole posse on the clifftop in one line. Like spraying flies with an aerosol. He was bloody cross by now, see. They all dropped off the cliff with the boulders still in their hands.' With dramatic timing, he re-lights his pipe with the lighter on full, until the smoke billows up. 'There was hell to pay that day. With his tail, he smashed their houses to matchwood and burnt the lot. There were people jumping off the cliff into the sea with their arses on fire, then drowning. *Bychan, bychan*, there's a place!'

'So what happened to the dragon then?' asks Gary.

'He opened up a Chinese on the island,' says Brian, 'and called it Dragon City.'

'Laughing aside,' says Harry in sepulchral tones, 'ever since that day, the dragon went into hiding, but whoever has tried to settle on the island since has failed. No word of a lie. Whatever was built in the day was found demolished the next morning.'

Everyone goes deadly quiet. All you can hear is the gentle lapping of the water against the sides of the boat. Gary has been looking periodically at the rock which guards the entrance to the harbour. Now he knows what it looks like. A dragon.

'Come on,' Brian breaks the silence. 'Let's get this heap of firewood on the road.'

As they head out of the harbour, Brian opens another tin of

beer and the froth goes everywhere. He swears, then slugs it back, beer dribbling down his neck. Then remembering Jim's instruction to make a noise, he goes over to his ghetto-blaster and switches it on, full volume.

'THE SUN AIN'T GONNA SHINE, ANY MORE!' it's an oldie. Brian gets a saw out of his tool set and starts strumming at it. Then he puts it down, picks up a chisel and starts singing loudly and out of tune into the handle.

'THE MOON AIN'T GONNA RISE, IN THE SKY …' Gwyn gets a diesel drum and beats on it with the wooden end of his trowel, serious concentration on his face. John is clashing a trowel and steel float together.

Harry pokes his head out of the wheelhouse, his face a mixture of concern and amusement. He hopes this isn't the start of a mutiny. The boat hits a patch of rough sea and Oar, who hasn't been holding on to anything, falls spread-eagled onto the deck, flat on his face.

'What's the matter with him?' asks Byron, 'he should be in his element here.'

'I wonder if it's possible to row with him,' muses Brian.

Scenting danger, Oar scrambles to regain his feet, but it's too late. They're on him. Next thing, one has his legs, one has his middle, and he's half over the side.

'Gerroff, gerroff,' he arches his back to keep his head out of the water.

'Come on boys, pack it in,' says Harry, stepping out of the wheelhouse. They haul Oar in and drop him. He flops like a mackerel onto the deck.

'Arrrrarrrr!' they shout together. Harry retreats into the wheelhouse as an empty beer tin flies towards him.

The harbour at Tairffynnon is at the mouth of the estuary. It used to be full of fishing boats and local fishermen. Now it's dominated by yachts and retired people, Captain Birdseye beards and denim caps. The squawking, swooping, scrounging, indiscriminately defecating gulls haven't changed though. Ian's shed is at the back, against the rock face. Inside is the milk boat. It sails right in every morning, depending on tides and awaits the arrival of the milk lorry. After it is emptied, the bulk tanks gets cleaned, then that evening, the cowman sails back to the island to do the next milking.

It's almost 7pm as a van reverses up to the side door of the shed. The back doors open and one-by-one, concealed by the doors, Gwyn, Brian and John leap in, just stopping short of dropping into the dark waters which slop around the boat. Stewart, the cowman, opens the stainless steel lid of the tank. They climb onto the boat.

'Come on, in you get.' His voice echoes round the watery shed. It's like climbing into a submarine. They've got torches, food, drink, everything. But it's a bit scary in there. And they haven't even hit the sea yet. It wouldn't do to imagine the boat going down. The whole space rings oddly when they talk, and they make squeaky metallic noises as they shift about. Then the engine starts and the tank reverberates. Brian claps his hands to his ears.

'Bloody hell, I can't handle this!'

'Don't shout!'

'I'm not shouting!'

'Who's farted?'

Then they hit the sea.

'Get off my foot!'

'I can't help it, I'm sliding.'

'Slide somewhere else, pal.'

'I think I'm getting claustrophobia.'

'Well don't give it to me.'

From his vantage point on the terrace of the Ship Inn, overlooking the harbour, Gary watches the boat going out. Hopefully, he alone knows that the tank on deck has got three bickering people inside. He has had chips in town for supper and called in for a beer to wash it down; now he goes in to get another drink to drown his disappointment at not being included.

As he emerges with his pint, he sees a girl sitting on her own reading, cool as you like, a few tables away. He recognises her immediately. It can only be one person. The one in the photo. Sarah Bowden. Her hair is different: plaited at the back, but it's her alright. His heart misses a beat. This time, he's smitten for real. She must be waiting for the others before making another sortie to the island. He frowns. That very night, she will probably be charged with criminal damage. Could she go to jail? She'll lose her job, whatever it is. And old man Bowden will never forgive her. Then he thinks of Brian manhandling her. That look on his face. Maybe he'll … no, he wouldn't would he? On an island in the dark with no one around? He must warn her not to go. He must. But how?

Right then, she gets up and walks, still cool and collected, into the pub. She's left her book and half-finished drink, so she isn't leaving. Gary gets out his carpenter's pencil and a scrap of paper from his wallet. He writes on it: 'DON'T GO TONIGHT,' then swiftly goes to her table and slips it under her drink. Just seconds later, he's downed his own drink and is walking rather hurriedly over to his car. Then he thinks, 'My God, what if the boys find out?' His forehead is coming out in a sweat. He's probably just ruined all their plans. It's too late to go back now. Confused and amazed by his own action, he gets into his car and, hands shaking, puts the keys in the ignition. Just then, a shadow comes across the dashboard. He looks up. It's her. She knocks on the window. He looks blank at her through the glass. She knocks again, more insistent. He gropes for the handle and winds the window down. She stares in.

'What d'you mean, don't go tonight?'

'Huh?' Gary's insides are turning like a washing machine on spin.

'What's this note?' She waves it under his chin. It's got a dark wet ring on it now.

'Not me.' That's all he can come up with. He feels like a foreigner, trying to speak English.

'Come on,' she says, raising her voice, 'I saw you put this under my drink.'

Gary swallows hard and looks into her face. It's not all anger there. There's puzzlement, bemusement and something else: a sparkle of interest.

'What's happening tonight?' she asks with strained patience. 'Who are you?'

There's nothing else for it. He blurts it all out.

'But it isn't us!' she insists. 'It isn't our way of going about things.' Then she reflects a little and says, 'At least I hope it isn't. If they're doing this behind my back!' She stands up straight and turns round, wondering what to do, looking very disturbed.

She looks in at Gary again. 'Don't go. I've left my book and handbag and I'm going to make a phone call. I'll be back in a tick.'

'Don't go!' thinks Gary. 'Try and make me.'

In a few minutes, she comes trotting back with her things and peers in at Gary. 'I can't get anyone on the phone. I'm going to go over to the island tonight, to see what's going on and make sure we don't get blamed for this. Are you coming with me?'

Coming with her! 'But how would we get to the island?'

'Swim. Can't you swim?'

The idea of swimming a freezing half-mile to the island in the darkness fills Gary with terror. He suddenly realises that this could be his last night on earth. He'll probably get cramp or something halfway and sink to the bottom. Gone without leaving a ripple. He may get a small mention in the Welsh News, but very brief: '... today a building worker drowned off Tairffynnon, and now here's the score in the rugby.'

'Ok,' he says trying to sound as nonchalant as possible, as if daring night-time swims are bread and butter to him. Then he feels her gaze on him and looks up to see that her eyes are smiling. It's the same mischievous smile in those bright blue eyes that he saw in the photo.

'Only joking,' she breezes, 'my father's got a rowing boat. Look, there it is.' She points to a brown, fibreglass dinghy moored to a yacht in the harbour.

She gets into Gary's car and they go first to Gary's house to get some warm clothes, then on to River View. Gary refuses to come into the bungalow. He won't even drive onto the property. He waits in the car for what seems like hours. Eventually she re-emerges. She's changed from shorts and tee-shirt to jeans and jumper. She's got a yellow waterproof coat, a blanket, a bag with food and a flask of soup in it. She's also brought a camera.

It's still light when they return to the harbour, so they go back to The Ship for a drink. 'A glass of red wine for me.' Sarah insists on giving him the money. They sit out on the terrace waiting for the light to fade. 'So which one are you?' she asks, with an inquisitive smile. 'There's one that Dad's really got it in for. He's got a streak through his hair. Dad says he looks like a savage.'

Gary smirks and looks into his beer. 'That was me, I'm afraid, I've changed my hair now.'

'You look pretty tame to me,' Sarah remarks, studying him closely. Her eyes are flickering like the lights reflected on the water behind her. 'So you're the one who put his foot through the ceiling?' Gary nods modestly and she laughs out loud. It's a mischievous, contagious laugh. Then she looks dark and disapproving:

'You don't strike me as a poacher.'

Gary looks awkward. He folds his arms, then puts his hands at the back of his head and leans back on the chair. 'I only went for the excitement, like. I wouldn't do it again.'

'I believe you,' she says.

Gary's worried about the dog now. What if she asks about the dog? Maybe she adored it.

'So whatever happened about Dad and Mum's dog?' she asks, as if on cue. Then, seeing Gary's look of panic, she adds: 'I never liked it anyway, I think they bought it as a substitute for me when I went to uni.'

'Poor substitute,' says Gary. What a gem. He's pleased with that one, and it's not a lie. She glows. He swears her to secrecy, then tells her the whole story about Tricksy's demise.

'She laughs with amazement. 'You people down here are very devious,' she says.

Out to sea, the island slowly loses all its detail until soon it's just a vague outline on the horizon. Darkness closes in and they're ready to leave.

'Where did you tell them you were going tonight?' Gary asks as they get up from the table.

'To an all-night beach party.'

'Now look who's devious.'

'How about you?'

'My mum wasn't home.'

They gather their things from the car and walk down to the quayside. 'Can you row?' Sarah asks.

'Well, a bit.'

'I'll row.' They untie the boat, throw all their things in, then Sarah gets in first and takes the oars. Gary climbs into the stern, wobbling the boat precariously.

'Careful.' She skilfully rows them out of the harbour, hardly having to look round. Thankfully, the sea is fairly calm, but it's chilly out there.

'Tairffynnon looks good from out here with all the lights,' says Gary, now in high spirits.

'Gary, could you sit in the middle, it's difficult to row.'

'Sorry.'

'We'd better not talk any more, sound travels across the water.'

'Sorry.'

'Ssssh.'

All that can be heard now is the gentle creak of the oars as they head through the dark waters. Gary starts to think about dragons. What if there really is some kind of creature yet to be discovered on the island? Another Loch Ness monster. Maybe that's what's knocked over the walls after all. He shivers.

It could already be lying in wait for them on the shore. He decides that he'll stuff an oar in its mouth and shout for Sarah to run while he grapples with it.

Ian's site on Ynys y Ddraig is looking like the stage set for an outdoor play, the type they have in castle grounds on summer nights. Stage right is the scrub, with low trees bent away from the wind; stage centre are the floor slabs at various levels with low block walls, like futuristic scenery, casting black shadows. Stage left, the ground falls towards the stream. The audience is one gentleman sat in a picnic chair against a tatty old tent with a floodlight mounted on it. He wears heavy outdoor clothes and a woolly cap pulled over his ears. There's a bottle of Scotch on the ground by his right arm, which hangs limply from the chair. He holds a baseball bat across his lap. He snores loudly.

Now a paramilitary-looking youth wearing a balaclava runs on stage right and starts pushing and kicking down walls. Immediately, there's a commotion from the edge of the scrub. Three men leap over a wire fence and rush towards the site. They try to catch the youth, but he darts this way and that like a rabbit, then sprints back for the fence and exits stage right into the darkness of the scrub. Three men blunder back over the fence and give chase. We hear voices off amid a lot of crashing of undergrowth and flickering of torchlights.

'Gerroff, it's me you stupid git, it's me Brian.'

'I seen him, he's over there, quick!'

'Ow my bloody head, owww!'

'Left, left, left, over there. Shit!'

The voices tail off into the distance. All goes quiet. Jim in the picnic chair continues to snore. He hasn't moved. Now an older man, also in a balaclava, appears from nowhere in the foreground, walks boldly onto the site and begins to push down walls. As he does so, a youth with close-cropped hair and a girl in a yellow waterproof top come on quietly stage left. The youth creeps up behind the man and rips off his balaclava while the girl takes a flash photo of him. He lunges for her, but as he does so, the youth rugby-tackles him onto the ground. He kicks the youth in the chest, gets to his feet and is about to deliver him a punch to the face when there is a loud crack as the girl hits him on the head with a piece of four by two. Instead of falling unconscious, he howls with pain, drops to the concrete and sits there, rocking back and fore, holding his head.

Jim in the picnic chair begins to stir, sees the commotion and leaps to his feet. Half-asleep, he stumbles down through the site, baseball bat in hand, looking confused. Three men re-appear and clamber over the fence stage right. They all group round the stricken man and look down at him.

'Obviously left the spinach behind,' growls Gwyn, picking the victim up by the scruff of the neck with one hand and lifting him to his feet. 'Popeye, my arse. 'Then he sees the blood. 'Who hit him over the head?'

'She did,' says Jim, pointing to Sarah, 'with a piece of four by two.'

Gwyn gives Sarah that puzzled look. 'Who's she with?'

'Me,' says Gary, without thinking.

'Give us the four by two,' Gwyn growls, 'and we'll make a proper job of it this time.'

'No, please no,' Popeye whines, half-choking with the tight grip round his collar.

'Better do some talking then, cos there'll be no talking after the lights go out, pal. Just tell us who's paid you.'

'What you going to do, are you going to report me?'

'Strictly in the family, as long as you spill the beans,' says Jim, 'but otherwise, we've got everything on video.'

Harry looks nervously about him, then he says: 'I gave her a lift, a while back, over to the island. She asked me what I thought of them building there and I told her straight: I hated the idea, but it was her and his land and they could do as they liked. Nothing to do with me.' He looks worriedly at the blood on his hands.

'Mrs Bartlet?' offers Jim.

He nods. Tentatively, he feels his head to make sure his skull hasn't caved in. 'Then she said she hated the idea too, her husband wouldn't listen and she would willingly pay someone to sabotage it.'

'Who's the other one who's with you?' asks Jim.

'Dafydd.'

'His son,' says Byron.

'Good, because you've both got some labouring to do in the morning.'

Brian saunters over to the tent and picks up the whisky bottle Jim had at his side. He opens the cap and smells it. 'Jim, you bugger' he shouts, 'this is real whisky.'

'I had to have something to keep me warm.'

'You really did go to sleep, no wonder you were no help.'

'Maybe for a second, but you were doing so well, I didn't want to interfere.'

Brian shoots him a reprimanding look and takes a deep swig at the bottle.

The Island Hotel is one of those tall Victorian seaside hotels that have seen better days. The render is cracked, the roof needs replacing, the list is endless. Fay's room has layer upon layer of floral wallpaper on the walls, which are spongy if you touch them. A large sash window, with folded bits of card wedged in here and there to stop it rattling, looks out towards the island. Fay always insists on coming here because she enjoys the decadence and thinks the owner is 'priceless' with her wheezy laugh and outrageous humour.

Ian walks in with his suitcase, whacked out after a scheduled flight from Florida, followed by a drive down from London. Fay is sitting by the window, the 'fallen angel', dragging nervously at a cigarette. No word is exchanged between them. He plonks his suitcase down, flops onto the bed and lies on his back with his hands behind his head.

Ian, being Ian, is amused by his wife's antics. But he's still a little shocked; and disappointed. 'I'm not angry with you,' he says eventually, looking up at the yellowing ceiling, 'but why darling? Why? Why didn't you just tell me you weren't happy about the house?' He turns his head in her direction. The hurt look.

Fay laughs in one abrupt exhalation of smoke. 'Oh come on, if I told you once, I told you a hundred times.'

'But I just thought ...'

'You just thought: typical woman, they're always moaning about something, probably the time of the month, she'll come round.'

'Yeah, maybe something like that,' he admits, with a boyish smile, 'but I don't understand, it'll be a great place to live, you'll love it.'

'Great for you maybe, you'll hardly be there. You'll be gallivanting round the world most of the time, for all I know having it off with other women ...'

'Oh, Fay!'

'… while I'm living on my own on that stupid island,' she glances through the window at it, 'getting bored out of my skull.'

'You can have people to stay, you'll have a whale of a time.'

'Oh come on, how many people are going to come to a remote, windswept, rainy island in the middle of winter?'

'I think it would have a certain appeal actually.'

She stubs the cigarette out decisively in the ashtray. 'Well, not to me. If I'm going to be abandoned for half the year, I would rather be somewhere where at least there are people around, not cows and bloody gulls.'

'Oh.' Ian is despondent for a full five seconds, then he perks up, 'I've seen a jolly good place for sale in Florida. Belongs to a friend of mine.'

She sighs. 'Poor Ian. The eternal nomad. When are you going to grow up and settle down? I'm English. My family is in England. So are yours as it happens.'

'Oh, sod them.' Then he sits up excitedly on the bed. 'Hey, you never guess what? I've bought an aeroplane!'

Harry Popeye's fishing boat is heading out of Tairffynnon harbour. This time, it has genuine day trippers on board. Among them young Gary and Sarah. It was all so simple. He bumped into her on the street a few days after their adventure and he asked her, joking really, if she would like to go on a day trip to Ynys y Ddraig. She said yes and here they are. A keen one for supplies, she's brought a bag full of food and drink.

'Fancy some crisps, Gary?'

'Yeah ok, thanks.' As he opens the packet, he looks round at the other passengers. He feels sorry for them in their mundane world from his vantage point in Nirvana. He's never felt so in tune with someone as he does with this girl.

'So what did you do in college?' he asks, gazing at her and plotting her features in his mind. Her hair is hanging loose today, blowing in the breeze.

'What course you mean?'

He nods, mouth full of crisps.

'Nature Conservation.'

He raises his eyes heavenward.

'You don't seem impressed. Don't you like the countryside?'

'Yeah, I suppose. But you don't say things like that round here. If I said "Isn't that a pretty view" to a bloke he would look funny at me.'

She laughs. 'It's interesting you should say that. That attitude could be what makes the countryside in west Wales so special. It isn't made to look like a picture book, people only do what's necessary.'

'Not too tidy and fussy like,' offers Gary. 'A bit more wild-looking. Yeah, I reckon I like it that way too.'

'Mind you,' she says, 'that same no-nonsense attitude is destroying the countryside as well. In the past, one man with a pick and shovel couldn't do that much harm in a day, but put that same man on a JCB now and there's no telling the damage he can do.'

'Maybe they'll take over.'

'What d'you mean?'

'Hey that would make a good film! The day of the JCBs.' He says it with a look of terror, eyes nearly popping out.

She pushes his arm with a giggle. 'Gary, stop it!'

But Gary is already absorbed. 'Suddenly, early one morning,

something takes control of all the JCBs in the country. They start coming to life, without drivers.' He raises one arm, like the arm of a JCB, and swings it round to her, making engine noises, opens his hand and grabs her shoulder.

'Gary don't!' she half-whispers, aware of the other passengers, then it's as if something tells her not to be so straight-laced and she changes her tune. 'So how does the film start?' she asks, eyes smiling, ready to hold him at bay if he strikes again.

'There's a couple lying in bed and the wife says, "Did you hear something, darling?"' Gary says this all posh. '"No, for God's sake, go back to sleep," says the husband. Next thing, a JCB bucket comes crashing through the window, glass everywhere, and pulls the whole wall out. Chhhh! The couple and their bed slide down to the floor below.'

'Gary, you're mad. What happens then?'

'There's a JCB going down a narrow road and meets a car coming the other way. The car driver gets really cross that he won't pull over. He stops the car and gets out, then he sees that there's no JCB driver. Aaaaaah!' Gary contorts his face with horror. 'Next thing, he watches his car being crunched to bits and shovelled over the hedge and the JCB just carries on. Soon the roads and motorways are full of JCBs, all headed towards London ...'

'Why are they going to London?' she interrupts.

Gary looks at her with mock anger. 'Give me a chance, woman, I haven't decided yet. This screenwriting is not easy you know.'

She laughs her infectious laugh, puts her arms round him and gives him a hug. 'I think you're going to be good for me,' she says. Gary likes the use of the future tense. He likes that a lot.

The boat is turning into the harbour at Ynys y Ddraig now. This trip doesn't go to the island, but Gary has persuaded Harry Popeye to drop them off *en route* and pick them up later. He was hardly going to argue. Gary points at the strange lump of rock as they pass. 'What's that remind you of?' he asks.

She studies it for a moment. 'Maybe a sea-horse or something.'

'A dragon?'

'Yes, I'll go for that.'

They disembark and as they walk up the path hand-in-hand, Gary tells Sarah the legend of the dragon. When he's finished, she stops and turns towards him. 'I bet you thought it was a dragon that was pulling down those walls, didn't you?' She shoves him playfully.

'Nonsense,' he says, 'otherwise why would I warn you not to come here that night?'

'You must have been pretty keen on me,' she suggests immodestly, 'to do that. Especially as you'd never met me before.'

'I seen you though, in a photo, with your bathing costume on,' he grins.

'What? Where?

'Not telling.'

They've come to Ian's ill-fated site. The job has been abandoned, at least for now. The dragon has won the day again. Grass will soon be creeping back over the concrete slabs; nature trying to heal the scar. Above the site, a small gate leads to a path through the scrub. They go through and Sarah sits on a half-collapsed dry-stone wall, surveying the view back over the valley and down to the harbour. The sun gives off a gentle warmth. The sky is blue, interspersed with billowy white clouds.

Gary goes off to have a pee. When he returns, she has her back to him, the outline of her shoulder blades and her backbone, like a string of beads, showing through her tee-shirt. He creeps up behind her, very close, then roars at the top of his voice, 'Rrrrrrrrrrrrh!'

She screams, leaps to her feet and runs forward a few paces.

'Thought you weren't afraid of dragons.'

'Gary, you bastard!' She runs at him and pummels his chest with her fists. He grabs her wrists, pulls her hands down to her sides and kisses her. She melts. They hardly know each-other, but somehow the time and place is right. Without another word, they peel off and dissolve as one into the 'not-too-tidy' landscape of Ynys y Ddraig.

6

LYDIA

They were nearly back at Putei now. The return journey from Moridunum had been long and arduous. Lydia's mother had died unexpectedly and Marcus, her husband had agreed to accompany her to her home, despite his obvious disquiet. In these unsettled times, it was dangerous to travel. Their armed guard, if anything, had made her more uneasy. Its very presence might provoke rather than deter attackers.

Marcus rode on his dappled grey stallion beside her carriage. He had been trying to hide his apprehension for her sake, but it showed in the lines on his face, his posture and the way he constantly fingered the handle of his sword. They were approaching the edge of a wood. She could feel the tension of the four soldiers who rode in front of the carriage and see it being transmitted to their horses, making them jumpy and light-footed. Beyond the woods was a village, an untidy sprinkling of wattle and thatched houses leading up from the estuary. The disciplined outlines of her family villa in the distance could at last be glimpsed through the trees to her left.

At a bend in the track, the soldiers came to a sudden halt and Marcus' horse reared up. Lydia leaned out to see what the matter was and gasped with horror. A group of savage-looking outlaws had materialised out of the trees like spirits. There must be about ten of them. Their clothing was rough and threadbare. Their eyes were cruel and taunting. They were armed with heavy swords and spears.

Lydia was gripped by a terror, the like of which she had never experienced before. For a moment, she was literally unable to move a muscle or even breathe. Then she remembered her mother's necklace and stubborn resolve absorbed some of her fear. They weren't going to get that. Bowing her head down low in the carriage, she quickly unclasped it and stuffed it in her mouth. At that moment, her husband leaned down towards her from his horse and whispered loudly, 'Run for it Lydia, run for the villa. Go now quickly, don't look back.'

There was no time to argue. Lifting up her cloak with one hand, she got down from the carriage as surreptitiously as she could, plunged into the woods and began running. Already, she could hear a din breaking out behind her and the clash of metal on metal.

One of them was pursuing her. She could hear snapping branches not far behind. She began to sob as she ran faster, and the breath stung like needles in her nose. Still, she kept her mouth tightly shut, concealing the precious necklace, which jangled against her teeth. He was gaining on her quickly; she couldn't bring herself to look round.

The villa was clearly visible now as the trees were thinning out. A few hundred paces of wasteland separated it from the wood. She even glimpsed slaves in the garden, beyond the perimeter wall. They might as well be a hundred miles away. Where was this god now? This god she had forsaken all others to worship? Would he save her?

A branch caught in her cloak and she tore at it in panic. She could smell her pursuer now. A rank smell. He was close, very close. Something struck her hard in the back of the spine. Her legs went numb and she fell to the ground, her head to one side in the dirt. He was standing over her, breathing heavily. Unable to move, too petrified to speak, she could only plead with her eyes. But as he raised the sword above his head, and their eyes met, his were cold and unmoved. Sobbing softly to herself, she closed her eyelids tight, vainly hoping that he would disappear like a bad dream.

Lydia's head had nearly been severed and the leaves and thorns were sprayed with her blood. Her killer was moving swiftly, pulling the spear from her back, stripping off her clothes, removing her bracelets, her belt, her rings, her purse. Then he had an urge to hide the corpse. Was it shame or fear of retribution? He began to drag it by the feet, the head hanging by a thread, to a rocky hollow in the ground. He rolled it in, capped it off with some large stones, before throwing smaller stones, soil and leaves on top.

WEST WALES 1990AD

The Welsh summer is living on borrowed time now. Almost patronisingly, people praise its capacity for survival. The trees have mellowed from a uniform green to a multitude of yellows and browns and blustery winds herald the onset of autumn; but still the days hold their warmth, though the mornings and evenings have become fresh, like a cold flannel across the face.

Jim is standing on his left leg in the dry base of a ditch, with his back to us. His right leg sticks out horizontally against the sloping bank. With both hands aloft, he holds the end of a cloth tape vertically above the centre of the ditch. His head is turned to the right, as he watches it being unwound.

Charlie, Jim's solicitor, is on the important end of the tape. He's showing Jim where the boundary of his latest bungalow should be in relation to the ditch. Charlie is casual, good-natured, ex-public school. He speaks English with a bit of a twang and Welsh with a lot of borrowed English words. His grey trousers are creased and shiny and his striped shirt is being pushed out by spare flesh at the sides. One tail of his tie has found its way over his right shoulder. He goes past the end of the bungalow, watching the numbers as he goes, then stops five feet across the front of the living room and digs his heel into the ground. He turns to Jim, nine feet away. 'You've definitely built part of this bungalow on land which isn't yours, I'm afraid. This is the boundary.' He points at his freshly-made dent in the ground.

Jim climbs out of the ditch and saunters over to take a closer look. 'I thought the ditch was the boundary,' he remarks, unconcerned, as if its Charlie's problem, not his.

'No, I told you when you bought the land, the boundary is actually nine feet in from the centre of the ditch.'

They both stare at the newly-finished building for a moment, as if willing it to move across a little, then Jim says, 'It could be a bit awkward if you have to climb over a fence to turn on the telly.'

'Not half,' Charlie agrees, 'especially if it's an electric fence and you're only wearing a dressing gown.' They both laugh heartily. 'And then what do you find? Sheep browsing in your bookcase. There we go, at least it's common land, you're not on anybody else's plot. You may not have to demolish part of the bungalow. You hope.'

Jim looks quizzically at Charlie for a moment, then asks, 'if you were employed to check the position of this boundary, where would you check it from?'

'The ditch of course.'

'Nowhere else?'

'It's an obvious physical feature.'

'Thank you,' says Jim meaningfully.

'Oar, go and get The Barbarian and tell him it's dinner time.' Brian kicks at his backside to send him on his way, before he settles on the floor in a corner of the nearly-completed living room to open his lunchbox.

'Gwyn doesn't wear a watch,' he mutters to John, 'they break with him after a couple of days.'

Gwyn is working on the JCB, in a belligerent mood. Jim has asked him to move a ditch across six feet from its present position. What's the point? On top of that, he's told him not to be fussy about it, not to make it too straight. His irritation is being transferred to the machine. He swings the arm over violently and drops a huge clod of soil into the old ditch, before punching it down with the back of the bucket. It's getting windy, and vegetation he's picking up is blowing about everywhere. As he swings the arm back to the new trench, he doesn't notice Oar.

Oar has been trying to attract Gwyn's attention, looking up into the cab and waving. When Gwyn sees him, his face registers startled surprise. He goes to reverse the controls but can only watch helpless as Oar puts out an arm to protect himself and ends up being neatly shoved into the new ditch. Gwyn stands and peeps down to see him land, frog-like, at the bottom. Then, almost immediately, he leaps up as if he's been

135

stung and scrambles out of the trench with a look of horror. He's standing at the edge now, cringing and pointing down at something.

In one motion, Gwyn swings open the door, climbs out of the cab and jumps to the ground. If there's a live cable Jim hasn't told him about, he's going to tear him limb from limb. But Oar is pointing at a cavity that's been partly uncovered at the bottom of the trench. Half-buried inside it, he glimpses something round and yellowy. From where he's stood, Gwyn assumes at first that it's a boulder, but then he sees the eye sockets.

Brian, Gary, Oar, Gwyn, Byron and Trevor stand round the trench looking down, like mourners round a grave. The wind rips at their clothing. The sky has gone slate grey, but a shaft of sunlight burns through and spotlights the area. John is below them, scraping at the soil with a trowel. Gwyn has removed several large stones to reveal a well-preserved skeleton set into a rock crevice, a crude natural tomb which runs slightly diagonally across the trench. The bones are half-submerged in a layer of fine, dark soil, which John is carefully removing. The skull is at an odd angle to the spine. It stares up blankly at six inquisitive heads.

'I bags that skull,' says Brian. 'It's going on my bedroom wall. Pass it up!' he shouts to John. John frowns. He doesn't want to disturb the skeleton. Who knows? It could be of archaeological importance. He ignores Brian and carries on revealing the ribcage. Impatient, Brian scrambles down into the trench, taking a minor avalanche with him. He goes round the front of John and with a finger in each eye socket, pulls the skull out of the ground. As he does so, there's a jingling noise and a stream of gold spills down from underneath it.

They gasp as Brian grabs his find and holds it aloft like a magician. 'Get a load of this!' The skull is forgotten. He hauls himself out of the trench, walks away a few yards and stops. Head bowed, he begins to examine it. The others crowd around him like eager schoolchildren. Every time they try and touch it, he snatches it out of reach and turns his body to shield it.

But they can see that he's holding a solid gold necklace as unblemished as the day it was last worn. There's a chain to go around the neck and the ornamental part is a series of rings inset with discs and linked together with short lengths of chain. You can tell that it's old because nothing is regular and machined.

John has come out of the trench now and they make way for him. 'Here comes the professor.' Brian hands him the necklace with some reluctance and he studies the discs, rubbing away any remnants of dirt with his finger. 'These are coins,' he says excitedly, 'Roman coins. You can read the writing. This one says H-A-D-R-I-A-N-U-S ... this necklace could be the best part of two thousand years old.' Their mouths gape open with childlike fascination.

'*Iesu Grist.*'

'That's fantastic, *ychan.*'

'It's like new.'

'That's gold for you. It doesn't rust, see.'

Each coin has an emperor's head looking to the right with a variety of images on the reverse. Brian grasps one of the coins, turns it over to face John. 'Come on then, smart-arse, who's this woman holding a dustbin lid?'

John examines it. 'That's Britannia, same as you used to get on the old pennies.'

137

'Oh.' He picks up another. 'There's an old geezer here with a beard, holding a harpoon gun. I've seen people with these in Majorca.'

'It's not a harpoon gun, it's a trident. That'll be Neptune, god of the sea.'

'Well I wonder why the dead man had a necklace in his mouth,' muses Byron, unfamiliar lines of puzzlement appearing on his face. 'Maybe he was a thief.'

'I think he was a she,' corrects John.

It hasn't occurred to anyone that the skeleton might have been a she. There's a pause while they re-adjust their mental picture of the long-deceased.

'Maybe the husband murdered her by sticking the necklace in her mouth,' suggests Gwyn.

Brian shakes his head sceptically. 'No point wasting a gold necklace, is there? A rag or anything would do. But if that's all that was handy, he would get it back, wouldn't he, if he had any sense.' Everyone nods gravely.

'I reckon she was a servant,' Gary suggests. 'She stole the necklace by putting it in her mouth, but then she choked on it and died.'

'No, I think she was mugged,' counters Oar. 'She put the necklace in her mouth so they didn't know she had it. They killed her and never found it.'

'Shaddup!' says Brian. 'Whaddo you know? One thing's for sure, it's worth a tidy bit. I'm getting a new car out of this.'

'Who says it's yours?'

'I found it, didn't I?' Brian grabs it back off John and guards it jealously.

Gwyn says, 'Don't forget who dug it up, pal,' in Brian's ear.

'Yeah,' shouts Oar excitedly. 'And I'm the one who spotted the skull.'

'And John uncovered it,' says Byron. 'Fair's fair isn't it?'

'Let's face it,' interrupts Gwyn, 'it belongs to all of us.'

'What about Jim?' Gary asks, 'He made you dig the trench.'

They all look at each-other.

'Jim can get stuffed,' says Brian tersely.

They fall silent for a moment. The sun has been extinguished, the wind has dropped quite suddenly and drops of rain are beginning to fall. A cloud has come over the boys too. Just ten minutes ago, their lives were simple. Now a few pieces of dazzling metal on a chain threaten to complicate things.

'So what do we do with it then?' asks Oar, almost despondent.

'Sell it and share the money,' says Brian.

'I think it should go to a museum,' John insists.

'Maybe we should put it back where it came from,' suggests Gary. He feels uneasy, that what they have done is a desecration of some kind.

Brian is dumbfounded. 'What? Put it back in the bloody ground? You can't be serious! This could be worth a bomb. Maybe we should bury you instead of it, you numbskull.'

Byron intercedes, exuding calm and reason. 'I suppose it wouldn't do any harm to find out what it's worth, anyway,' he says, tipping his head to one side, as if to welcome any contradiction. Intuitively, he's found the middle ground. Nobody objects to this idea.

'There's only one more thing to settle now,' says Trevor, looking down thoughtfully and kicking the grass with the tip of his foot. 'Who's going to look after it?

'I will,' says Brian without hesitation.'

Oar, standing at a safe distance says, 'How do we know you won't sell it yourself and buy a car?'

Brian says nothing. With a look of resign, disgust and disappointment, he places the necklace on the JCB and gets a penknife from his pocket. Then deftly, he begins to break the necklace apart so that each coin has a short length of chain to go with it. The gold is soft, so it isn't difficult. 'I don't know if anyone's noticed,' he says, 'but there's seven of us and seven coins.'

John is flabbergasted. 'What are you doing? That could be priceless. I don't believe it!'

Brian turns to him, hands on hip. 'We might not have found this at all, so where's the problem?'

'Well, we have, so now it's our responsibility. At least remember what order they're in.'

'No problem. Mine's the one with these horses on the back. Oar, you can have the one with the tripod, whatever it's called …' he hands them out like pieces of chocolate bar.

Jim's latest bungalow has got an attic room with an en-suite bathroom, so that the owners can say they've got a dormer bungalow. The plans showed a dormer window, but Jim couldn't be bothered with that (they always seem to leak with him), so he's changed it for a rooflight. The room has been plasterboarded and Gary is in the middle of fixing skirtings.

'Hi Gary.'

He turns round and sees Sarah at the top of the new stair, lighting up the room. He smiles from ear to ear, drops his hammer, goes over to her and gives her a lingering kiss.

'You're all covered in sawdust,' she exclaims, 'and you smell all woody.'

'What d'you expect, I'm a carpenter.'

'Where's Brian?'

'On another job.'

'So this is where you work.'

'Today, yes, I work wherever the work is.'

'Yes, I suppose you do, silly me.'

'So what room is this?' she asks, clomping across the chipboard floor.

Gary is flushed, a little embarrassed that she's here, but delighted to see her. 'This is a bedroom and next-door is an en-suite bathroom. '

She opens the rooflight and looks out. 'Not a bad view.' Then she closes it again, turns round and spots something on the plasterboarded wall to the bathroom. She goes over for a closer look. Gary shuffles about awkwardly.

'My God, this is amazing!' She crouches to see more of the detail, then stands back to look at the whole picture. Someone has drawn a sketch, a sort of cartoon, in carpenter's pencil, on the plasterboard wall. There are seven men, in a circle, all pulling at the same necklace. The lines of power are striking. The necklace has just broken and they are all going to fall over backwards. The surprised faces are all slightly caricatured. Sarah instantly recognises those she has met, including Gary himself. In the background is a shadowy, faintly-drawn figure of a woman in swirling clothes. She looks indignant.

'This is brilliant! Who drew this?' Gary shrugs. He says nothing.

'Gary! You drew this, didn't you? I can't get over you sometimes. I didn't even know you could draw.'

'It's crap. I was just pissing about. The sooner that walls gets skimmed the better.' He shrugs again.

'Well, if this is crap, I look forward to seeing your good work, that's all I can say.'

Gary changes the subject. 'So are you going to north Wales this weekend? For your protest thing?'

'Yes, that's partly why I called. Are you coming?'

He puts his finger to his lips and talks in a whisper. 'Yes, but I don't want the others to know. They'll think I'm getting in with a bunch of hippies.'

'Hippies!' she stares at him in anger.

'Sssh! That's what they'll think. They'll think I'm going to nest up a tree all weekend.'

'But we are, and we have to dress up as birds.'

'Forget it!' He flicks his hand up dismissively and walks away. 'For-bloody-get it!'

'Gaaaaary!'

'What?'

'Only joking.' She's wearing her mischievous eyes. 'It's only placards and speeches.'

He spins round, waves an admonishing finger at her, before flashing her a forgiving smile. 'I would like to see you in action.'

'You will.'

'I'll be going up to London as well this week, for a building exhibition.'

'I know.'

'You do understand, don't you, it's a kind of work thing, all blokes like. Otherwise I would ask you to come along.'

'Don't be silly Gary, of course I understand.'

'A bit colder today, isn't it?' Trevor remarks to the man opposite, who ignores him and carries on reading his newspaper. The train rattles through the tunnel like a loose bullet in the barrel of a gun, then slows down dramatically as they blast into another underground station. It halts abruptly, the doors thud open, a mass of people pours on and they judder off again, gathering speed.

'Funny people,' says Trevor, turning to Brian, 'look at them, they just stand there looking all blank, like. I reckon you'd get a better conversation in a cattle truck.'

'My gran told me they used to talk to each-other in the war,' says Oar, shifting a scrawny pair of knees to one side as someone brushes past, 'but after the war ended, they soon went back to being odd like this again.'

'I don't blame 'em,' says Brian. 'There's that many nutters and weirdos about, it's best not to talk to anyone.'

'This is the station!' They leap to their feet, but the doors open on the other side. There's a huge scrum in the way.

'Excuse me!' says Brian. Nobody takes any notice. 'Excuse me! Can we get off here please?' Again nobody makes an effort to move.

Gwyn puts his hands together and wedges them into the crowd. Then, with a perfect breast-stroke action, he forces a huge swathe of humanity to the left and right of him in two squawking, indignant, stumbling, protesting arcs. 'Baaastards!' he mutters, and stomps off the train. The others follow, laughing, in his wake.

As the elevators push them relentlessly upward on a wave of draughty warm air, Gary imagines that they are all particles of sick, diced carrot maybe, being regurgitated from the bowels of the earth. A slow-motion vomit. But he doesn't bother to share that thought with anyone.

The boys all seem so different. Brian is wearing a shell-suit and he slithers about with a good-natured air. Trevor has got his hair slicked back, denim top and trousers, pointy shoes. Obviously ahead of some fashion revival. Gwyn is wearing a striped suit and tie, but the bottoms of his trousers are all bunched up round his shoes, a sure sign that beneath his jacket, the bum-cleavage lurks. Oar looks as if he's been washed and spun in his clothes and hung out to dry.

The building exhibition is their excuse for a day off. They don't spend too long there. Few of the reps have any practical experience of building. All they can do is spout theory. So they stuff themselves with vol-au-vents and white wine, sail past the stalls, before bursting back out into the afternoon air. There is, after all, another reason for their trip to London.

'Are you absolutely sure you want to part with it, madam?' asks Mr Willoughby, eyeing the sapphire and gold ring through a magnifying glass. He has a weakness for sapphire. When this example has been polished up, it will offer a magical glimpse of the ocean depths. 'It's exquisite.'

'I know, I know, please don't. It's difficult enough for me as it is.' Seeking consolation, she strokes the miniature poodle, which twitches nervously on her shoulder. It wags a ribboned tail and sinks deeper into the fur coat. Then it tenses up again as a bunch of unlikely-looking individuals stumbles noisily into the shop.

Seeing the counter occupied, the new arrivals peer at the jewellery on display in several cabinets, leaving finger marks all over the polished glass. Up on the ceiling, a camera follows them closely.

'Get a load of this, I bet that's worth a bob or two.'

'Hey, look at these pearls by here.'

'They're diamonds you dingbat, pearls are round.'

'Look at the size of those earrings. *Duw, Duw,* solid gold. Imagine the weight, boy. Any woman wearing these, it would nearly rip her lugholes off.'

'It's Arabs buy things like this I reckon. They're the ones with the money, see. There's some would think nothing about buying stuff like 'is.'

'I just seen one on the way here, wearing all the gear like he just came off his camel.'

'They don't have camels, *ychan,* they have Mercs with tinted windows.'

'Aye, mos' prob'ly he was a diplomat.'

Mr Willoughby looks a little concerned by his new customers. He presses a hidden button and a wraith-like figure appears next to him.

'Can I help you gentlemen?' asks the new apparition, throwing his voice out onto the shop floor.

'Yes,' says Brian, swishing over to the counter. 'Can you value something for us?'

'It rather depends what it is.'

Brian reaches into his pocket and produces his share of the necklace. He places it on the counter.

'I see.'

'No, you don't. This is only part of it.' He half-turns. 'John!' John brings forward his contribution and one by one they come forward and place their discs in order on the counter, recreating the necklace. Gwyn is the last. As he places the image of the emperor Antoninus Pius on the counter, along with a length of chain, the shopkeeper is visibly taken aback by the thickness of his fingers.

'Well, gentlemen,' he says warily, 'a very significant find.

It is definitely Roman. Rather a pity that it's in pieces. Never mind, one assumes that it can be re-assembled. Might I ask why it was taken apart?'

'It belongs to all of us,' grunts Gwyn, by way of an explanation.

'I see, well I only hope you don't all share a car.' He smirks, then flinches as he meets with a wall of silence. Gwyn doesn't like this shop assistant. There's something superior about him. He gets the urge to put a pair of hands round his skinny neck and squeeze until his eyes pop out.

Very cautiously, the assistant now proceeds to pick up the discs individually and peer at them through a magnifying glass. 'These coins are gold *aurei*. Depending on their condition and rarity, as individual coins, they might fetch anything from one to ten thousand pounds apiece.'

'*Iessssu Grist!*'

'*Duuuw, Duw!*'

'But as to the value of the complete necklace, I would be reluctant to guess.' He pauses and raises his eyebrows enquiringly, ill-concealed suspicion on his face. 'Might I ask you how you came about this?'

They shift about uneasily, looking at one another.

'What part of Wales are you from?' he ventures, appearing to be very interested, as if they might be a rare breed of penguin.

'A part where people are very cagey about answering questions,' Brian retorts. 'This necklace has not been stolen, it belongs to us.'

'I'm guessing you dug it up whilst doing building work.'

'Maybe, maybe not.'

'I don't know whether you are aware of common law with

regard to treasure trove,' the man continues, trying to regain the upper hand. 'The coroner needs to be informed. My advice is that you contact your county archaeological department and they will advise you on how to proceed so that you are not breaking the law. All things being equal, you should gain financially from this item. But it all takes a while.'

'Are you thinking what I'm thinking?' says Brian, turning to Gwyn.

'I'm thinking Jim. We're going to have to bring Jim into this.'

'Fraid so.'

As they shuffle out of the shop, the assistant barks at their retreating backs, 'whatever you do, don't try and sell the necklace privately. You could end up as guests of Her Majesty.'

Out on the street, Oar pipes up, 'I don't get it. Why would we be staying with the Queen?'

'This is the place. Here, pull in here.'

'Yes, ma'am.' Gary turns his red Fiesta into a car park overhung with trees. It's been a few hours' drive up to North Wales. He and Sarah get out and stretch their limbs for a moment. With all the rain over the last few days, everything is looking tired and soggy, but the sun is starting to show through.

Cars hiss by at speed on the wet tarmac as they walk single file onto a stone bridge. The bridge has Vs in the parapet walls to shield pedestrians from the traffic. You can see where the stonework has been re-built after minor accidents. There's a roaring noise to their left where water plummets down from a high waterfall thirty yards upstream. They stand in one of the Vs and gaze up at it. It's almost alive, the way the foam bounces this way and that with the changing flow, never the same, always taking on a different shape. The air is filled with a fine spray. They both shiver.

Not surprisingly, the waterfall has become a tourist attraction. Overlooking it, almost carved into the rock, is a quaint collection of stone Victorian buildings: a hotel, a pub with a beer garden and climbing frame for children, a gift shop, a restored mill and a private house. It's still busy even now in autumn time.

'Let's cross the road,' Sarah suggests. They pause while a lorry thunders past, before crossing hurriedly to a V opposite. Downstream, the gorge widens dramatically and the river meanders at a leisurely pace through green meadows. A few men fish off the riverbank below.

'So,' says Gary, what's all the fuss about?'

'Would you believe, they want to build a flyover right across this valley, on columns.' Her face takes on a faraway look that Gary hasn't seen before. She points to the top of the steep bank. 'That's where it's going to start, then it's going right over to there. See where that copper beech is?' She traces a line through the air with her finger. 'Pistyll has become a bit of a bottle-neck and they reckon the narrow bridge, the dip and the bend are dangerous. They're going to by-pass it.'

Gary frowns. 'Can't they just widen the bridge?'

'That's what we're pushing for. Either that or taking the new road up-river where it's hidden more and the bridge can be smaller. '

'You're organising the protest then?'

'Yes, vaguely. Me and one or two others, I suppose.'

It's 11am as they drive into the nearby village, a neat collection of cottages built with boulders so massive that you can count the number of stones to each front wall. The village hall is in cut stone with pointed arched windows and a steep roof. They turn into its car park and pull up next to a battered camper van painted in several colours.

'Hi Sarah! Who's your friend?' comes a voice from behind them as they walk in.

'Maggie, this is Gary.'

Maggie offers him a hand from underneath a pile of boards and papers and nearly drops the lot. She is a little overweight and pants with exertion, exuding equal doses of sweat and enthusiasm. 'What branch are you from, Gary?' she asks, hurriedly retrieving her hand.

Gary looks flustered and angry for a moment. They are perching up trees after all. Then he realises what she means. 'I'm not a member.'

'I hope you join. We need all the support we can get.' She shuffles off and they follow her into the hall. It's a hive of activity, the tables covered with half-completed placards. Earnest-looking individuals dip paintbrushes into a few communal pots and print in large, sloppy letters onto rolls of paper.

Sarah does a sort of royal tour. Everyone seems to know her. 'Nice one, Gerry. A BRIDGE TOO FAR. Maybe you could thicken the lettering up a bit.'

'Ok thanks.' He pecks her on the cheek. Gary feels a twinge of jealousy.

'What's this, Jamie? ANOTHER CONCRETE JUNGLE BUGLE. What's the idea of the bugle?'

Jamie looks at her, puzzled, stroking his Charles I beard,

then looks down at his placard. 'Oh bother, I missed out the N.'

'Isn't there anyone local here?' whispers Gary when they've been round everyone.'

'Most of them are local.'

'I haven't heard a North Wales accent since I've been here.'

Sarah isn't listening. She's thinking about the placards. 'It's ok,' she says, but it needs that extra oomph, know what I mean?' She looks distractedly at him for a minute, half-looking through him, then her eyes widen. She pokes him with a finger and he steps back, bemused.

'I know exactly what it needs,' she exclaims, staring at him with an enigmatic smile. 'It needs a drawing by the maestro, that's what it needs.'

'No way,' protests Gary, 'no way am I doing any drawing.'

There's a perfect view of the old bridge from where Gary sits on a yellow coat on the grass. He's been given a large sheet of paper on a plywood backing, leant against a fence, and some marker pens. They've dumped him here and abandoned him for an hour to produce a drawing. Just ahead and to his right is where the new bridge is to start. It's hard to imagine all that traffic flying through what is now fresh air and landing over on the other side of the valley. He decides to draw it just like that. He won't draw the new bridge at all, just the traffic crossing the valley in mid-air. Anyway, he's not quite sure what the new bridge will look like.

It's quite still when Gary starts to draw. All he can hear is the rumble of distant traffic. But soon his presence is forgotten. Birds re-settle in the trees and the undergrowth once more rustles into life. He drifts into a kind of trance, lost in his work and his surroundings. At one point, a fox bursts into view just twenty yards away. It spots Gary, turns its head and stares motionless at him for some time before slinking off across a field. He draws it in.

'Gary, that's amazing!'

He turns, and there's Sarah. Like the fox, she's been watching him, motionless, for some time from a patch of raised ground behind him. There's something timeless, something permanent about her solid stance, with the autumn sun outlining her features in gold. He memorises the image.

'Bloody hell, my arse is numb.'

She bends over him, a hand on each shoulder, her face next to his, and drinks in the drawing. Then she stands back a bit. 'What a brilliant idea not to show the new bridge at all, just all that traffic hurtling through the air. It looks like it's being spewed out of a massive pipe just off the picture.' She comes forward again to study the detail. 'I love the smoke belching from that lorry. Boy, you've made these cars really aggressive. And the valley, the old bridge, the buildings and the waterfall, they look idyllic. Gary, it's a gem.' She squeezes his shoulder.

He turns his head and smiles warmly at her. She looks tense. 'What's the matter?'

'I've got to make a speech.'

'I know,'

'You will be there with me, won't you?' She shivers a little.

'Of course I will. Where else d'you think I'll be.'

They've worked the protest so that the traffic is hardly held up at all. If you're trying to win people over, Sarah says, it's no good annoying them by creating a huge traffic jam. As vehicles approach the bridge, they run a very tame gauntlet of protesters standing with their placards on both sides. At the bridge itself, Gary's picture has pride of place, with the caption: IS THIS HOW YOU WANT PISTYLL TO LOOK? Gently, drivers are brought to a halt and offered a leaflet.

At about 4pm a big TV van arrives, and the protesters congregate in the car park. By now, a throng of locals has materialised and the air is filled with the distinctive nasal sound of North Wales Welsh.

As soon as Gary sees the TV cameras, he scampers off like a rabbit and hides behind several heads, to avoid even the remotest chance of anyone at home seeing him on the Welsh News. From his hideout, he watches Sarah as they help her onto the bonnet of an old Renault and hand her a microphone. How can she stand there in front of all those people and cameras with no crib-sheet or anything?

At first, she looks a little flustered and distracted, but she soon gets into the swing.

'... How many of you even knew until today that a huge flyover on stilts was planned for this valley?' She waves a finger around the crowd. 'Practically the first inkling you'd have had would be traffic lights and mysterious excavations going on in the field over there. That's the way they want it. They don't want you to know. Move in fast before Joe Public has a chance to argue.'

Gary feels enormously proud. That's my girlfriend, he thinks, standing up there, dead confident, in front of all those people. She seems very angry. It scares him a little. But it's sort of controlled. A lot of politicians bark and snap at you, he thinks, but she doesn't. You want to listen. And you believe what you hear.

She outlines the problem as the Highways Department see

it and explains exactly what is proposed. She argues that the flyover is a ridiculous over-reaction; a waste of public money. The existing road can easily be improved and the bridge widened. Otherwise, a tourist attraction will be spoilt and a lot of livelihoods affected.

'... so it's up to you,' she concludes, pointing that finger again. If you don't stand up to them, they'll just walk all over you. You'll end up crying over spilt milk. It'll be too late, the damage will be done.'

As she gets down from the car bonnet, Gary wants to go and congratulate her, but a flock of reporters and members of the public crowds in. He feels that it's her moment, so he holds back.

Soon the crowds disperse. Cars are leaving. The demonstration is at an end. But where's Sarah? His eye scans the rapidly diminishing crowd. No sign of her. Maybe she's in his car. But when he gets to it, she's not there. She must have gone off for an interview or something. Heavy at heart, he drives back to the village hall.

The car park there is almost deserted. As soon as he goes to the door, Maggie emerges with all her paraphernalia. He smiles briefly and brushes past her into the building. Empty. He re-emerges and calls weakly after her retreating figure. 'Have you seen Sarah?'

'Yeah,' Maggie shouts over her shoulder. 'She's had a lift down south with Mick and Deidre. Didn't you know?'

Gary feels as if someone has stuck a giant syringe into his stomach and sucked all his insides out. He sits down heavily on the boundary wall of the yard, with his back against the fence. He can't believe it. He can't comprehend it. She's gone.

The kitchen of the dormer bungalow has become the venue for an impromptu gathering. The boys stand solemn-faced with their backs to the half-fitted units. Trevor puffs at his pipe, coughs profusely, opens the back door and spits flamboyantly into space. Brian is playing with the unconnected taps in the sink. On, off. On, off. The loose worktop behind Gwyn moves back suddenly with his weight, putting him off balance. He turns round angrily as if to punish it.

'I've talked to the archaeology people,' says Jim, running his finger across the blade of a chisel he's absent-mindedly picked up. 'They want to see the necklace and the find has to be reported. So what d'you say, boys? I think it's time we handed it in.'

Breaking up the necklace has given each 'shareholder' the power of veto. Whatever decision they take now has to be unanimous, otherwise it will never be re-assembled. Silently, they mull over whether or not to trust Jim. Presently, John comes forward, wallet in hand, takes out his disc and places it on the newly-fitted breakfast-bar where Jim is standing. Gary follows suit. But Brian stands stubbornly with his back to the sink, his hands planted firmly on the draining boards to each side of him. 'How much can we get for it?'

'Nobody knows that, but if it isn't reported, there's likely to be trouble. And then maybe we'll get nothing. We don't have much choice. We need to put it back together and hand it in.'

Byron and Gwyn put their discs on the table, then Trevor, then Oar. They do so a little mournfully, as if parting with a friend. Everyone is looking at Brian now. Finally, with a sigh of resign, he comes forward and starts fitting them together, introducing his own as he does so.

As soon as the necklace is complete again, Jim picks it up

and says: 'of course I should mention that it does actually belong to me, since it was found on my land.'

'Wuuuuh!'

'No bloody way it doesn't!'

'Pull the other one, Jim!'

Gwyn is wearing his bovine look. 'P'raps we should look into exactly whose land that ditch is on, Jim.'

'Yeaaaah!'

'Too bloody right!'

Jim smiles a naughty-schoolboy-who's-been-found-out smile. 'Yes, there could be a problem there. It would be safer really if the skeleton was in the back garden here. They've got an archaeologist who wants to come and look at it. Maybe you found it while digging a soakaway, Gwyn.'

'That can be arranged, Mr Davies. Eight equal shares of whatever money we get?'

'Jim nods.'

After 1,724 years, Lydia is being moved from her resting place. In stages from the top down. John has carefully laid out her top half in the base of the barrow, but Oar hits a bump on the way over, and her ribs and vertebrae get jumbled about a bit, leaving Brian with a headache to reassemble them in the new hole. But he soon has her sorted out ready to receive the arms which come rolling over on the second barrow-load.

In no time at all, the skeleton has been re-assembled. It looks very convincing. They all stand looking down at it with admiration as Brian shakes a last bit of soil round the bones, then climbs out of the trench himself to have a look.

'No, fair play,' says Byron, 'that looks really tidy, honest to God.'

'I reckon she would be proud of it herself,' says Oar.

'Maybe you could get a job in a museum,' Trevor suggests, 'putting dinosaurs together. I bet there's money in that.'

It's a couple of days later in the bungalow garden. Scratching noises emanate from a circle of bunting and steel posts which surround the soakaway hole. At the base of the hole, a man on his hands and knees scrapes away diligently at the soil with a trowel. He wears a lumberjack jacket, corduroy trousers and a puzzled look.

Someone comes out of the bungalow a few yards away and starts washing out a bucket that had pink plaster in it. Then he goes back in again. It's odd, thinks the archaeologist, that he doesn't come over for a nose. It's odd really that none of the others do. Then he notices something about the skeleton. He scrapes some more. Soon, he spots something else. Slowly, the puzzled look on his face changes to a broad smile.

The next time he glances up, Mr Davies the builder is looking down at him from behind the bunting. Mr Davies looks fascinated by what is going on. 'What have you found so far?' he asks earnestly.

'Well,' says the archaeologist, 'we can already say for sure that the deceased was quite a remarkable person. She must have had considerable difficulty overcoming her physical problems.'

'Goodness me, what was the matter with her?'

'Well, for a start, she had four fingers on her left hand and six on her right. Several of her vertebrae were also the wrong way round.'

'Good Lord!' says Jim, alarm bells ringing.

'But here's the really remarkable bit. The top half of her was facing one way and the bottom half the other.'

Jim tries to express astonishment, while starting to look for a hole of his own to crawl into.

'Do you know what that means?' asks the archaeologist rhetorically. 'It means that she had a choice of either seeing where she was coming from and walking forwards, or seeing where she was going to and walking backwards. It's quite possible that she had wing mirrors, but I haven't found any yet.' He starts to laugh then and once he starts, he goes into uncontrollable spasms, crouched in the hole, holding his stomach. This sets Jim off and the two men, complete strangers, howl with mirth for several minutes, nearly recover, then start each other off again for another spell.

Presently, as they both stand outside the bunting, wiping tears from their eyes, the archaeologist says, 'Dear me, I haven't had such a laugh in years. So what really happened here?'

Jim concocts an embarrassed look. 'I'm afraid the boys removed the skeleton to complete the soakaway. I made them put it back,' he lies. 'Only they didn't do a very good job of it. Unfortunately, they've made a muck of your evidence.'

'It is a pity that we can no longer record it in situ, but all is not lost. The important bits have survived: the skeleton and the necklace. Hopefully, the local museum might eventually be able to acquire the necklace and display it with the skeleton.'

It's a foul night. Gary is home alone and there's been a power cut. He sits in the parlour, hunched up on the settee. A wood fire blazes in the hearth and a solitary candle burns in a saucer on the table in front of him. They both cast conflicting shadows on the ceiling. Outside, the wind worries at the window. Cold draughts sneak through the room, hugging the floor as they seek out the fireplace.

Gary's eyebrows are knitted into a deep frown. He's thinking, thinking; searching back through events, trying to work out how he might have upset Sarah.

A huge gust of wind thumps against the front door, flicking dust and leaves into the hall. The candle blows out, but the fire bursts into life, flames reaching high and sparks spitting everywhere from the fresh off-cuts. Tomorrow it's Saturday. Shit or bust, he's going to talk to her.

'I never liked him from the start, clumsy young oaf,' says Mr Bowden. 'I'm a pretty good judge of character.'

Mrs Bowden gently scolds him. 'Nonsense, dear. He's a sweetie.' She turns to Sarah. 'I wish you'd talk to him. Poor chap. He keeps phoning. He must be desperate.'

Sarah says nothing. She's got to escape. She's feeling boxed in. She reaches for a coat, puts it on and tucks all her hair under the collar at the back. Then she wraps a scarf hurriedly round her neck and flies out of the door.

She has to start putting him out of her mind, she decides, as she pulls out onto the road in her mum's car and heads for town. She was fooling herself into thinking they could ever be that close. Their backgrounds are too different. It's a losing battle. She's going to buy a new coat, that's what she's going to do.

She rounds the corner and slams on the brakes as a streak of red comes right across her path. She closes her eyes, waiting for the bump. When she opens them again, she sees that it's Gary. Damn it, she's having a job stopping herself from smiling, she's so pleased to see him. He's getting out of his car now. She can see that she's hurt him. He looks all squeezed out like a dishcloth.

'Gary, for God's sake, move that bloody car off the road.'

'You won't drive off?'

'I won't drive off.'

They both pull into the quarry and park side by side. Gary gets into the car beside her. 'I don't get it,' he whines, slamming the door, 'what have I done to you?'

She stares fixedly ahead, watching a pile of leaves swirl in an eddy of wind against the rock face. She grips the steering wheel in both hands, fighting back tears. 'Where were you, Gary? You promised. You promised you'd be with me when I did my speech.'

'I was there for God's sake, I was a few yards away. I watched you do your speech. You were brilliant,' he says gloomily.

This seems to satisfy her for a moment, then she darkens again. 'Yes, but you weren't *with* me.' She slams her hand on the steering wheel and turns towards him with bitter eyes. 'You're ashamed of me. That's what it is, isn't it? You don't want to be associated with fringy student protesters like me. I'm just another hippy to you.'

Gary looks gobstruck. 'I was proud of you, if you want to know. I only hid because they were swinging those bloody cameras all over the place.'

'Yes, and you didn't want to be seen with me.' She's confused now. She isn't sure any more herself why she was offended. Did she want him there to impress him or for his support?

'And afterwards, you kept well away from me, didn't you?'

'I didn't want to get in the way. There were so many reporters and things around you.' He's tongue-tied, too stewed up to argue. He wants to say that he didn't have to endorse everything she did. It was one thing to help her, another to be her puppet.

'I helped you, didn't I? Anyway, I didn't think you needed anyone to hold your hand, you seemed so kind of ... sure of yourself, like.'

Sarah bows her head over the steering wheel with her arms folded. Damn it, why doesn't she climb down and say sorry to him? All things considered, she's been an unbelievable shit.

'Yes, you did help me, thank-you Gary,' she says with great effort. 'I was over-reacting, it was just that you weren't there, or rather I didn't see you there, when I needed you.'

'Sorry, I don't like cameras. Can we be friends now?'

'Yes.' She looks down, ashamed.

'You won't leave me like that again?'

She's straining every sinew now, struggling to fight off the Bowden pride. 'Sorry,' she says finally, almost inaudibly, 'and no, I won't leave you like that again. Shall we go somewhere?' she suggests wearily.

'My mum's gone to Cardiff for the weekend,' says Gary with a mischievous grin.

Eight months have passed. The boys have been well rewarded for the find and Lydia has been moved yet again. Now she's behind a glass case in the museum at Tairffynnon. The skeleton has been re-assembled and the necklace is displayed flowing from her mouth. Not strictly accurate, but it would hardly be impressive viewing hidden inside the skull.

The description shows enlarged photos of all the coins, states which emperors they represent and explains the images on the reverse. It's suggested that she fell victim to robbers.

'I don't like it,' says Gary. 'I wouldn't like my bones to be on display in some museum.'

'I know, it's as if she's naked,' says Sarah. 'It's indecent somehow, what d'you think Sue?'

Sue shrugs. 'She's been dead a long time, does it matter anymore? Anyway, you're not exactly recognisable like that.'

'I want to be cremated when I die, and my ashes used for fertiliser,' Trevor announces.

'Weedkiller more like.' Brian pushes him towards the door. 'Come on, let's go. I could murder a pint and there won't be any remains left of that.'

As they drift out, Sue sidles up to Gary. 'Sarah has told me that you're a talented artist.'

Gary gives her a pained look, willing her to be quiet, afraid they'll be overheard.

'She says she's been nagging you to do an art course for months. Now I am too. You'll have some money now, that'll help.

Gary looks flustered and embarrassed. 'I don't know ...'

'If I had half your talent I would, 'she says, scolding him. 'Don't waste it.

7

WHEN MY BOAT COMES IN

Porthwen was one of those ports on the west coast which had no harbour. The sloops used to beach themselves, unload in low tide and could sail off again, weather permitting, on the next tide. There's an old black and white photo on the wall in the cafe showing the beach in the foreground with several of those big boats, slightly tipped to one side. Horses, carts and people are milling around them. In the background are rows of white houses, some even with white roofs. In fact, everything in Porthwen seemed to have been painted white, including low walls and the base of trees even. There used to be a saying on the west coast: 'Stay in Porthwen the night and you'll come away white.'

But all that has changed. The beach now throngs with tourists in summer and the village retains little of the magic of yesteryear. The front is a mish mash of flat roofs, tarmac, ice-cream signs and wasp-infested dustbins. A disused lime-kiln hugs the rock face, stinking of urine, partly overgrown with brambles and obscured by boats of all shapes and sizes. Nearby, a heavily-rusted old tractor is used for towing them up a concrete slipway.

The old buildings sit uneasily beside the new, like disapproving parents, although most of them too have lost their dignity to flat render and gaping windows. The frivolous converted railway carriages on the hillside have far more appeal, but here and there, you can still spot an old building in the village that has slipped through the ruthless net of modernisation.

There's one in particular: a little bakehouse, like a miniature cottage with two windows each side of a central door, a large stone chimney and a little upper gable window. Could its days be numbered? Graham is standing outside it now, clip-pad in one hand and measuring tape in the other. Jim trots up to join him from the car park. The door of the little building opens and out steps Mike Sotheby-James. Mike is 'County Family'. He was brought up in one of the local mansions. It has now been sold off, but he still owns a few properties. This little bakehouse is in the yard of Captain's House, a three-storey house of his, which looks over the sea.

They walk in. It's quite cold inside. They have to step down onto the quarry-tiled floor because the yard has been built up over the years. Graham raises an eyebrow. 'Can't get a lot in here.' Within the two-foot thick walls, there's just one room with a low beamed ceiling and a large stone ingle-nook. Inside this is a bread oven and, in the corner, a large cauldron within a low wall and a little grate set in below it. The funnel-shaped chimney, a miracle in stone, tunnels its way up to a bright square of sky above. To the side of the inglenook, there's a built-in boarded larder with a low door. 'So what did you want to do with it?'

'A holiday flat I was thinking,' replies Mike. 'I reckon it could be rather nice.'

Jim waves a dismissive arm towards the inglenook. 'We could pull that lot down for a start.' He pushes towards it with both hands as if that might be enough to knock it over. 'That would give you quite a bit more room.'

'No no no,' interjects Mike. 'We won't be knocking things down.' You can almost hear the little building breathe a sigh of relief. 'The inglenook is what makes the building.'

'But you are going to need a kitchen, a bathroom and where are people going to sleep?' asks Graham, with knitted brows.

'You can make an opening in the gable at the side of the inglenook and build a lean-to for the kitchen and bathroom. They won't be large, but that's ok.'

'But what about a bedroom?'

'Upstairs.'

'What upstairs?'

Mike raps the ceiling boards with his knuckles. 'There's a room up there, or so they say. It's all closed off now, but there was definitely a stair. See these trimmers coming across here?'

'Funny they've blocked it off,' says Graham, 'you'd have thought it would be used for storage.'

'They say that's where the Captain's housekeeper lived. They also say that there was more than just a ... how should I put it ... professional relationship.'

'When was that?'

'Maybe 1850s. A good while ago.'

'Can we open it up?' asks Graham, 'so that I can measure.'

'That's exactly what I was hoping to do, I would be fascinated to see up there.'

'I think I've got a nail bar in the boot,' says Jim.

'No need,' says Mike. He goes across to a shed attached to

the big house and after a bit of scraping and crashing, returns with an aluminium ladder, a nail bar and a hammer and cold chisel. Jim takes the nail bar and starts prising away boards with ominous splintering noises.

'Go easy!' shouts Mike. He can see he's going to have to keep an eye on Jim. He had to employ him because his sister is married to Jim's wife's brother. He would rather not have.

'*Ych a fi*, you can go up there,' says Jim, 'I'm staying down here.' He hands the nail bar to Graham. 'Use this for the cobwebs.'

Pushing his head up through the opening, Graham feels a mixture of unease and excitement, like an Egyptologist who has discovered a tomb. It's obvious that the room has been shut off for a long time. It's very dark up here; the gable window has been boarded over, allowing only the narrowest slivers of light to come through. The air is thick with cobwebs. Through them, he can make out two items of furniture: a wooden home-made box bed and a chest of drawers. Both very basic. Presumably, they were made in situ, because they couldn't have been carried up through that small opening.

The room is low; nearly all in the roof. Graham has to stoop to avoid the A-frames. He fights his way through the cobwebs using the nail bar like a machete and crosses to the window. The floor is sprinkled with dead and buzzing flies and chunks of lime plaster, which crunch under foot.

Michael pops his head up through the opening and gazes around. 'Wow, that's amazing!'

The gable window is almost on the floor. The first board takes some prizing loose. But once it is removed, it's easy to get the nail bar behind the others. As they come away, mounds of flies pour down and light blazes in. Graham peers through the dirty glass. There's a good view of the sea, in fact this view alone might ensure summer bookings. People will always pay to look over that infinite grey wetness, he thinks.

'There's a good view over the sea,' he says over his shoulder, but there's no reply. He turns round, 'I said there's a ...' he stops, puzzled. He could have sworn that Michael had come up and was right behind him. But now he can hear him downstairs, talking to Jim. He shivers. It's quite cold up here, considering it's under the roof. But he argues it is a cloudy day. He measures up hurriedly, clearing more cobwebs in the process, and scrambles back down through the opening in the floor.

It's a few months and several yards of red tape later and Jim's boys are working on the bakehouse. It's midsummer. The gable lean-to is more or less up. Its roof is being felt and battened.

'Down tools! Dinner time! Let's hit the beach man!' Brian's hammer rattles on to the scaffold. Gwyn sticks his head out of a new window opening. 'It's only ten to.'

Brian says: 'Near enough, it's time for a swim.'

'I got no trunks,' moans Oar.

'No problem.'

'It's a baking hot, clear day. Everything is bathed in glistening, silvery light. Porthwen is swarming with tourists, cars everywhere. Brian, Gwyn, Gary and Oar descend to the beach down a narrow road bordered with double yellow lines. Kids in bare feet walk crane-like up the warm tarmac towards them carrying footballs, frisbees and surf boards.

'I got no trunks,' says Oar again, trotting to catch up with Brian.

'Shaddup will you, quit moanin.'

When they get to the front, the noise hits them.

'Maaami, Philip hit me!' blubs a kid in front of them.

'Mummy, those horrid boys are kicking sand in my eyes!'

'Nigel's stolen my bathers!'

They veer over to the right side of the beach, against the rocks. Gwyn finds a little shaded enclave which he fits into perfectly. He sits on the sand with his back to the rock and reaches into his haversack for his sandwiches and tabloid.

Gary's struggling with a towel, but Brian simply peels off. He's already wearing his trunks. He starts jumping on the spot, impatient. 'Let's go go go!'

'I got no trunks,' whines Oar.

'Jeeeesus! Wear your underpants!' says Brian, then looks away with a smirk.

'I can't do that. People will notice.'

'Don't be daft, I done it loads of times. They don't look any different. To be honest, I don't know why I'm bothering with trunks.'

'Nor me neither. I often wear my pants to go for a swim,' lies Gary, hating himself.

Looking round him nervously, Oar strips off and scores of tourist marvel to see a pallid beanpole in bright red Y-fronts. Brian and Gary sprint for the sea.

'Hey, wait for me!'

It's a little later. Gary is sunbathing whilst eating his sandwiches. He's making a concerted effort to go bronze this year, but somehow it isn't working. He's coming out in red blotches.

Brian has been joined by Derek, who is working on a bungalow at the back of the car park. Derek is very tidy and complete. He wears tidy overalls to work and he keeps his tools tidy. He talks tidy and he acts tidy as long as you're tidy with him. Even now, wearing only his trunks and devoid of any props, he still manages to sit tidy. The two have been stalking two tourist girls ten yards away. They rise to their feet now like predatory lions and head for the kill.

'Here comes the Baywatch team,' mutters Sandra, parting her long, jet-black hair. She rises reluctantly to the sitting position.

'Damn, I was just going to have a read,' says Fiona, pouting. She rubs Factor 6 on her shoulders. Bloody typical.'

'Can we join you?' asks Derek politely.

'Looks like you have,' says Fiona.

Brian sinks down into the sand, no hands, ending up cross-legged. 'I reckon I know where you girls come from.'

'Aw yeh?'

'Yeh, Birmingham. I like the accent,' he lies.

'And I reckon you two are natives. Where's the spears?' she teases.

'I've got a Spear and Jackson plane,' offers Derek.

'And he's got war paint,' says Fiona, cheekily pointing at a tattoo on Brian's shoulder. It's a lot of squiggly lines, a heart and the name Helen. Brian goes defensive and covers it with his hand. Helen ditched him on a holiday in Spain. It was the shame of coming back alone that bothered him most.

Sandra changes the subject. 'Carpenters are you?'

'No, we're lifeguards.'

'Not much cop then,' she says, 'you're facing the wrong way, someone could have drowned and you wouldn't know it.'

'We've got eyes in the back of our heads,' explains Derek.

'We've got a sixth sense,' adds Brian. 'We can tell if

someone is drowning without even looking. You city people wouldn't understand,' he says, holding his hands out in mock exasperation.

'You don't have to come from the country to recognise bullshit when you see it,' Fiona retorts. The girls laugh together, forming a momentary wall, excluding the boys.

'You girls seen all the sights then?' asks Brian, ploughing on.

Fiona smirks, 'Oh yeah.'

'You need some locals to show you round,' insists Derek.

'What?' she grins, looking past them. 'Like him?'

They look round and Brian groans. There, not three yards away, stands Oar in his red Y-fronts. They've become two-tone. The darker bottom half indicates the exact depth he has ventured into the sea. His goose-pimpled legs rattle together.

'Jesus, Oar,' says Brian, 'get some trousers on.'

But Oar isn't listening. He's looking back up at the bakehouse. 'Did you lock the door?

'Gwyn did,' grumps Brian, looking away in disgust.

'Well, who's that woman in the window?'

'What window?'

'The pine end window.'

'There's nobody in the window. Get some trousers on.'

Sandra's looking now. 'Is it that little white building? I can see her. She's looking out to sea.' Sandra's following her gaze, but there's nothing to see except a sailing boat way out on the horizon.

'You're both nuts,' says Brian, angry that he can't see anything. 'Where?'

'She's gone now,' they reply in unison.

Ten minutes later, Gwyn and Oar walk up the road from the

beach, an odd pair: together they make two, but the dividing line is way off-centre.

They pause for breath when they reach the bakehouse. It's breezy all of a sudden. The sun has gone in and the water out to sea is all churned up. The leaves are showing their backs on the ash tree nearby. The door is definitely locked. Gwyn turns the key and a little cautiously they walk in.

Almost immediately, they hear footsteps cross the attic above them. 'Must be some kid,' says Gwyn. 'I must have locked him in. I'll go up and fish him out.'

'It's not a kid,' Oar insists, 'it's a woman.'

Gwyn climbs up the aluminium ladder. 'Come on out of there, whoever you are, you won't be harmed.' Then the floor joists creak alarmingly as he stomps overhead. A minute later, Oar sees his feet re-appear on the ladder and slowly descend. When he emerges, his face is a picture of puzzlement. 'There's nobody there.'

'Did you look behind the chest of drawers?'

'And in the box bed. There's nobody there.'

'Maybe they went out through the window.'

'It's a fixed light. It doesn't open.' He stares at Oar. In those few seconds, Gwyn seems to have changed. He seems to have shrunk in size. Gone is the craggy confidence. It's the child Gwyn. 'There's nobody there,' he says again in a lost voice.

Oar is sniffing now, ferretlike. 'Can you smell bread?'

'Yes, I think I can,' says Gwyn, 'now you come to mention it. 'Fresh bread.'

It's a few days later. They're hacking off plaster from the internal walls.

'Sometimes,' says John,' you can hear noises from

somewhere else, as if they're in the room. It's like they're ... projected ... into the room. My neighbour's got a house built against a bank with a field above. Sometimes, and I swear this is true, because I've heard it: the fireplace moos like a cow. Yes, it does. The noise comes straight down the chimney from the field above.'

'I'm telling you now,' Gwyn insists, 'the noise was up there.' He points steadfastly at the ceiling. 'It wasn't from anywhere else. I know what I heard. You can think what you ...' then as if on cue, footsteps can be heard above, going towards the gable. They freeze.

Oar sneers at John. 'From somewhere else is it? Projected is it?'

'Sssssh!' Gwyn puts his fingers to his lips, shoulders hunched. Stock still, dead silent, they listen, breathing sparsely. Presently, the footsteps come towards them across the length of the loft. Three heads with ping-pong eyes turn to follow the sound. Footsteps are heard slowly descending. Oar is standing in the middle of the room, his head swivelling round, eyes staring. Then he starts to sway back and fore before his knees give way and he collapses on the floor like a bundle of rags.

When he opens his eyes again, he sees distorted figures in black and white looking down at him. He feels like every ounce of blood has been sucked out of him. 'Am I dead?'

'No.'

'Are you dead?'

'No Oar, nobody is dead. You fainted.'

Oar gets shakily to his feet like a new-born calf. Still muzzy, he sits back down on a pile of cement bags. 'I seen her,' he says, shaking his head to clear his thoughts. 'I seen her like I'm seeing you now.' The boys form a shocked horseshoe of attentive faces round him. 'She was walking on air. Walking on bloody air, until she got down to the floor.' He pauses, hunting for breath, then to his surprise, finds that they remain motionless, waiting for him, Oar to resume. 'Honest to God. Sometimes I could only see part of her, like she was chopped across the middle. That's the most incredible thing I've ever seen. Weird man, weird.'

'What did she look like, Oar?'

'I don't know, very short, with her hair parted in the middle and tied round the back in a ...'

'Bun?'

'Yeah, bun. She had a shawl round her, all colours, and a browny dress right down to her feet. She came towards me at one point, man that really scared me. There's something else ... she was pregnant I think.'

'I definitely saw something moving,' says Gwyn, pale as death. 'Definitely, I saw something move across there. And we all heard it.' He looks sternly at John, challenging him to deny it. And I tell you something else.'

'What?'

He sniffs at the air. 'I can smell that bread again. This place is bloody haunted. Spooked out. We need danger money to work here.'

Brian, who has just come in with Gary, scoffs. 'Well, I ain't seen or heard nothing.'

Gary looks disappointed. 'Nor me neither.'

'I never believed people before,' says Gwyn. His head seems to have retreated, tortoise-like, into his shoulders. 'I thought ghosts and stuff was all bullshit. But now I know different. How are we going to carry on working here with this ... woman wandering about the place?'

Oar is outside now. Trance-like, wobbly-legged. He gazes out to sea. Sure enough, way out on the horizon, he sees the big white sails of a yacht. He comes back inside. 'I think know what causes it,' he announces, 'she walks whenever there's a sail on the horizon.'

'So when the weather is too rough, maybe we'll get some peace,' says Gwyn.

'Or too calm,' says Oar.

For the rest of that week, the weather is dead calm and no sails are seen out to sea. Mike, the owner, is working on site wearing very old, tattered clothes. Brian calls him the posh tramp. He's set up a Workmate bench in the yard and is repairing the windows. He could do them in his workshop, but he is hoping one of Jim's boys will be interested. He's right. Both Gary and Oar stop for a nose whenever they get a chance. He's put a new sill in the left-hand window and pieced in the bottoms of the jambs with a sort of Z-joint, the top and bottom cuts sloping down and outwards. He's got the opening light on the bench now. He's taken the glass out and chiselled off all the old putty.

'See these four dowels? If I take them out, the window should come apart. The bottom two dowels are very soft, but he has to tap the top two sharply. 'Here you go.' With the gentle help of a wooden mallet, the whole window comes apart. 'Now I just repair the rotted bits and put it back together again.'

'Where did you learn to do all this?' asks Oar.

'When we had the mansion, a joiner came to repair the windows. There were a lot of them. He started to show me how to do things, but I'll never be as good as him, you could hardly spot some of his joints. When I asked him what the secret was, he just said, "You have to keep your tools sharp." He was right.'

'I'm not sure Brian sharpens any tools,' observes Gary. 'He just buys a new hardpoint saw and uses an electric planer. We sharpen our chisels, I suppose, but that's about it.'

'Jim wanted to put plastic windows in,' says Oar.

Mike screws up his nose. 'I know. There's no hope for him.'

'Jim is a bungalow man,' says Gary, surprised to find himself almost defending him.

'What about the gable window? Does that need doing?' asks Oar.

'Well yes … I started on it, but …' he seems reluctant to say any more.

'You had a bad feeling,' says Oar, 'and you left it.'

Mike shoots him a 'How did you know?' look.

'Tools down! Dinner time!' shouts Brian. This time, he is a full quarter-of-an-hour early.

'When Jim gets wind, he'll be here every day at one,' mutters Oar, turning to Gary. He looks round. No Gary.

Gary tentatively pushes open the entrance door of the Further Education Centre. He has finally plucked up the courage to enquire about art courses. Ahead of him is a long, wide passageway with glossy white brick walls. Part-way down, there's a hatch with a sliding glass window and a sign above which reads 'Enquiries'. Furtively, he creeps along the vinyl-tiled floor, hoping not to bump into anyone on the way.

Just when he's on the point of resting his elbows on the narrow sill of the hatch, a door further down bursts open noisily. Out spills a class of future brickies. They flood towards him in a boisterous tidal wave. Hurriedly, he crosses the passage and begins to scan the notice board opposite as they pass.

'Hello Gary.'

Gary glances round. 'Hello, Tony.'

'What are you doing here?'

'Er, just waiting for someone.'

The flood subsides and the passage is empty once more. Gary turns and stands with his back to the noticeboard, summoning the courage to cross. He can hear Sarah's voice nagging in his ear. 'Go on Gary, ask her. Ask her what art courses they do. Go on, ask her now.'

He goes over to the hatch, looking cautiously to his left and right as if he's crossing a main road. Inside, a woman has her back to him and she's making scores of photocopies. He raises his hand to knock on the glass, but doesn't like to disturb her. He lowers it. Then another door bursts open.

This time, it's carpenters. He can smell the wood on them.

'Hello, Gary, you teaching now, are you?'

'Yeah, sure.'

'Hello Gar, what you doing here?'

'Oh what the hell.' He joins the flow and leaves the building with them.'

Towards the end of the week, a breeze picks up in Porthwen and the boys get nervous. John is hacking off the inglenook walls. Gwyn is repairing some loose tiles on the quarry-tiled floor, which is to be kept, and Oar and Gary are plasterboarding between the joists of the ceiling. Brian is out flashing the lean-to roof. Oar glances out of the window and says: 'sailing boat on the horizon!'

Immediately, there is a mass exodus. They flood out onto the yard like frightened mice, as if it's a fire practice. They look at each-other, despondent.

'It can't carry on like this,' says Gwyn.

'There's only one way of sorting this out,' says Oar authoritatively, 'have a séance.'

Gwyn looks sideways at him. 'Wassat?'

'When you communicate with the spirits,' explains John, with a distinct lack of conviction.

'My aunty did them,' continues Oar.' My dad said she talked to that many spirits, she was like a bloody telephone exchange.'

Brian scoffs from up on the lean-to roof. 'I'm not sitting round no table holding hands with anyone,' he shouts.

Gary grins. 'I want to see them going all weird and talking in funny voices and shaking and stuff. Yeh, and what's this ectoplasm look like?'

Oar shakes his head emphatically. 'No, it wasn't like that. All my aunty had was an upside-down glass on the table and letters all round. It works, honest to God it does.'

'Crap,' says Brian laconically.

Gwyn stares at him. 'You don't have to join in if you don't want to.'

'If you don't believe, better you don't come at all,' adds Oar.

Brian looks pensive. 'I was only joking,' he says, backtracking. 'Why don't we do it tonight?'

'Women are good for making it work,' says Oar. 'It always works better with women.'

'No way would Peggy come,' says Gwyn.

'I'm not coming either,' says John.

'Sarah is away,' says Gary.

'Don't worry,' says Brian, 'I'll go and ask Sue dinner time.'

Sue lives in a rented flat on the first floor of a converted old warehouse near the harbour. A flight of stone steps leads up and round to the door at the gable end. Brian takes the steps two at a time with a smile on his face. When he rings the doorbell, the door will fly open and she'll drag him into her domain like a trapdoor spider to be consumed.

'Brrrring!' No answer. As he goes to knock on the door, it opens slowly. She's stood there, wearing an apron, blocking the door opening, arms folded, insipid look on her face.

Brian, left standing outside, looks taken aback. 'What's with the face like you've just eaten shit?'

'I haven't eaten it, Brian, but maybe I'm looking at it.'

'That's a bit 'arsh, what have I done now?'

She pauses for a second, gathering her thoughts. 'I don't know why you've bothered to come here, Brian, I really don't, there's plenty more fish for you in the sea, or should I say, on the beach.'

Cogs begin to whirr in Brian's head. One of her friends must have spotted him chatting to those girls on the beach. But he may be wrong, so he asks, 'What exactly do you mean?'

'Come on, Brian, you were seen talking to those Brummie girls on the beach.'

Bloomin 'eck, she even knows where they come from, there must be a whole dossier on him.

'What a fuss, I was just passing the time with them.'

'Why didn't you pass the time with some blokes?'

He smiles his winning smile. 'They were easier on the eye, I suppose.' He puts his arm around her waist and leans forward to kiss her. She bats him away with the palms of her hands on his shoulders. 'No, Brian!' she shouts.

Brian looks round to see if there's anyone near. 'There's no need to shout.'

'And you put your arm round one of them, with them not wearing very much, just passing the time I suppose.'

Brian gets defensive. 'I seen you chatting to Gary, you looked pretty friendly then I reckon.'

'Of course I'm going to chat to Gary, what do you think I'm going to do, ignore him?'

'I reckon you fancied him.'

'Gary has got Sarah.'

'It was before that.'

Sue thinks, yes, maybe she missed the boat there. But she's glad he's got Sarah. He seems happy. 'Not everyone is like you, Brian,' she retorts.

'I know,' he says, pretending to turn it into a compliment, and starts to paw at her again.

'Gerroff! I don't know where you've been.'

That seems to hit below the belt. His face turns dark. He feels angry and humiliated. For a second, she thinks he's going to strike her, but he just spins round and starts to stomp back down the steps. 'Bitch!' he mutters to himself and bangs the side of his fist on the tubular handrail. Pwong! He hurts his hand.

'I heard what you said!' comes a voice behind him from the top of the steps. Something flies past him and flops down the last few steps below him. It's a toy sheep he bought her at the Royal Welsh.

'Baaaad shot,' he quips to himself without smiling.

When Brian arrives back, Gary can see straight away that

something is wrong, but nobody else seems to notice. 'Sue can't come,' he says breezily, 'but I think I know just the ones who can.' A broad grin spreads across his face. 'We'll call in The Sloop after work. You can bet they'll be there.'

The Sloop Inn is almost empty; in between busy times. A shaft of late afternoon sunlight, a constellation of sparkling dust, streams in through the front window and divides the room in two like a curtain. Jim's boys troop in through it, undergoing a momentary transfiguration as the particles whirl around in frantic eddies. A man in shorts and a loud short-sleeved shirt sits on a stool by the bar as they queue for their drinks. He's got a wide mouth, round canine eyes and a shallow forehead. A fag burns idly in his cupped hand.

'You lads working on that little house up the road?' His voice has a self-satisfied purr to it. 'You wouldn't get away with scaffolding like that back home, would you Sid?' He twists round to Sid, who is sat next to a large television which mutters to itself in the corner.

Sid cocks his head to one side. 'Come again, Dave?'

'Ah say, they wouldn't get away with scaffolding like that back home, would they?'

Sid's got a podgy face and his cheeks quiver like a bulldog's when he shakes his head. 'Aaaw, naaaw.'

'Mind you, this is a smashing village,' continues Dave. 'Now don't get me wrong, a bit backward maybe, but the potential is there, no doubt about it.'

'Potential for what?' growls Brian, confrontational. His right hand on the bar, concealed by Gary, is clenched into a fist.

'It's your infrastructure that's important, isn't it Sid?'

'Aw yeh, definitely.'

'What I mean by infrastructure,' Dave explains carefully, 'is your proper road and rail network. Once you've established that, then everything else follows.'

'Like what?' asks Brian, hands on hips, chin raised.

Dave takes a drag from his cigarette and exhales theatrically. 'I've been dealing with people all my life. All sorts. I can sum anyone up at a glance. I can see you're not stupid. We've talked to some smart people while we've been down here, and I mean local Welsh people, haven't we Sid?'

'Surprisingly smart, yeh.'

'All that's needed here is a helping hand, a kick-start, so to speak.'

'What he needs is a kick in the arse,' mutters Gwyn.

'Now with improved communications,' Dave drones on, 'that little place you're working on – now don't get me wrong, I'm sure you lads will do a pucker job – no straight up, I mean it sincerely, but with improved communications as I say, that could be a five-storey hotel with balconies overlooking the sea, the business. And that's just one property. You could have a marina here and water sports, amusements, miniature railway, you name it. No doubt about it, this place could really take off. Instead of a few die-hards like me and Sid, you could have literally thousands coming here.'

'I can't wait,' says Gwyn, turning to order his drink.

Just then, Sandra and Fiona walk in. The boys surround them like wasps round a jam pot.

'We need your services,' says Brian.

Fiona looks daggers at him. 'Bog off!'

'We'll pay for it,' says Gary.

'In drinks,' says Oar.

Sandra looks bemused at Brian. 'Come on, let's have it. What's going on? What you after?'

They edge the girls out of earshot, hurriedly procure one G and T and a Bacardi and Coke, then Brian says in a creepy voice, 'We're going to summon up the dark forces.'

'Ooooh!'

'It's just a séance,' corrects Oar breezily.

'I been to one of them, it were right scary,' says Sandra. 'Ooh, I don't know.' Then she looks suspicious. 'Why d'you want *us*?'

'It works better with women,' explains Oar.

'Come on,' says Fiona, thinking of the free drinks, 'it's our last night, it'll be a laff.'

Sandra looks wide-eyed. 'Is that place you're working on really haunted like?'

'Yeah, he's seen her again,' says Gary, nudging Oar.

'She probably fancies him,' says Fiona, 'after seeing him in those Y-fronts, that's why she was looking out of that window I reckon.'

'Ok,' says Gwyn, deadpan. 'We meet back here at 7.30pm, agreed?'

At around 7.30, Gwyn, Gary, Oar and Brian return in dribs and drabs, looking fed, scrubbed and polished. Sandra and Fiona are several drinks down the line. They greet them all like old friends. 'Hi lads!'

'We need a table,' says Gwyn, when they've all assembled. And some chairs. 'What about this one, Oar?'

'This one's better. It's bigger and more shiny.'

Gwyn shouts to Tom behind the bar. 'We're borrowing this table and some chairs.'

'And mind you return them', shouts Tom at their disappearing backs, as they struggle out with all the furniture. He wipes down the bar with a hopeless shrug.

A strange procession travels the fifty yards from The Sloop to the bakehouse, along a patched and wonky tarmac road lined with tall houses and scented gardens which follows the contour of the hill. Gwyn leads with the table. The boys follow in a line carrying chairs. Sandra and Fiona take up the rear with the drinks. They giggle together and an impromptu cocktail of spilled alcohol swills around the two trays they're carrying.

It's already quite gloomy inside the bakehouse when they cautiously unlock the front door and stumble in. The plaster has been hacked off the walls. It's like a room in a ruined castle.

'It's getting dark in here,' says Gwyn, struggling in with the table.

'Ssssh!'

Gwyn looks puzzled. 'Why do we have to whisper?'

Nobody knows.

'I'll go and turn on the electric,' suggests Gary. He returns two minutes later with a paraffin lamp. 'Mike is out and I can't get in the house. But he left this in the shed for emergencies. We've never used it.' The olive green metal is all greasy with paraffin and it stinks, but they greet it with rapture. They crowd around eagerly and light it, then they hang it proudly from a nail on the ceiling, where it shines with a comforting glow, casting flickering shadows and giving off wisps of smelly smoke.

'What now?' asks Gwyn, setting up the chairs and table.

'We have to make letters,' says Oar. 'Bugger it, we haven't got any paper.' He frowns and scans the room.

'What about an empty cement sack?' Gary suggests.

'That'll do.' They cut a sack into little squares with a Stanley knife and someone produces a carpenter's pencil.

'What do we write?'

A to Z. 0 1 2 3 ... to 9. YES and NO. They arrange the little squares of paper round the table in a circle and place a small, upturned glass in the centre.

'We'd better block off the windows,' says Brian. He doesn't want to be seen. He finds two more empty cement bags and jams them in the windows.

'Cor, it's creepy now,' says Sandra.

The participants finally take their seats. As instructed, each places a tentative finger on the glass. They lapse into a deathly silence. You can just hear the sea and the faint thud of a jukebox in The Sloop. Above them, the lamp spits and crackles. The smell of paraffin is all-pervading. Eerie, ever-changing shadows mingle on the floor and ceiling and a large round blob of a shadow from the base of the lamp swings back and fore across the table.

Oar looks heavenwards with a strange expectant look. 'Is there anybody there?' he asks the air in a sepulchral voice. Fiona erupts into fits of giggles and immediately infects Sandra. Inadvertently, they blow half the letters off the table. Gary and Brian start laughing. The whole event looks like turning into a farce.

Gwyn growls at them. 'What's the point of this if you can't be serious?' Cowering with guilt, they re-arrange the letters and start again.

Oar repeats the question, and without a second's delay, the

glass moves to YES. They follow its movement wide-eyed. Everyone is concentrating now.

'What's your name?'

G W E N. The glass moves rapidly from one letter to another, like a dog straining on a leash. They have trouble keeping up.

'What work did you do?'

H O U S E K E E P E R.

'Where?'

B I G H O U S E. They read out the letters together aloud like children in nursery school.

'Next-door?'

Y E S.

'Who lived there?'

C A P T A I N.

'Are you with him now?'

N O.

'No?'

W A I T I N G.

'Waiting for him? Where is he?'

S E A.

'At sea.'

M A R R Y M E.

That explains it,' says Oar. 'That explains why she walks whenever she sees a sail on the horizon. It sets her off, like. She thinks it's him coming back.'

'To marry her,' says Sandra.

'Maybe that's when she starts baking bread,' Gwyn suggests.

Oar has a hunch and asks: 'How did you die, Gwen?'

C H I L D B I R T H.

'That's so sad,' says Sandra, 'and now she's just waiting and waiting. I wonder what happened to him. It's awful. We've got to help her. He won't come now, Gwen,' she says, feeling foolish about conversing with fresh air. The glass begins to revolve. Round and round it goes, squeaking almost pathetically as it scrapes the surface of the table.

'You have to go and join him now,' says Oar, 'go to the light.' Gradually, the glass grinds to a halt. They keep their fingers in place, not daring to breathe for several seconds, then Oar asks: 'are you still there, Gwen?' The glass begins to move, slowly and painfully towards G. Then it goes to A R Y.

'Gary! It's talking to Gary!'

'It's someone different,' observes Oar. 'The movement is different. Who's this?'

A N N I E.

My God, thinks Gary, it's Mrs Alexiou. Can that be possible? Yet there's something so normal about it. Suddenly, she's there, large as life. Yet she isn't. It's hard to fathom.

'Have you got a message for Gary?' asks Oar.

Slowly, but surely, it spells out A 1 0. A10? What on earth is that? Then Gary remembers. It's a room in the Further Education Centre. As soon as he realises this, the glass moves again.

M O N 9 3 0.

Gary grasps it immediately. Monday at 9.30. But he begins to have cold feet. The glass moves again.

G O.

'What's all that about, Gary?'

'I dunno. Doesn't make sense,' he lies.

Gary is outside Jim's house in Hafn Derwen. How's he going to take this? As he's about to knock, the door opens and Jim brings him into the nerve centre, a room with a table in the middle covered with papers. There are shelves on two walls, bulging with files and over-filled large envelopes, some of which teeter on the brink of falling to the ground. All kinds of building samples lean against the walls, including a cut-away plastic window.

Gary begins to explain himself: 'I ...' but before he can say anything, Jim whispers, 'Get down!' A car has pulled up in the yard. Gary crouches down, puzzled, and sees Jim on the floor on all fours. 'Head for the escape capsule!' he whispers. Gary joins him on all fours, and the two of them quickly crawl, like babies who have not yet learnt to walk, towards a windowless storeroom. Jim nudges open the door with his head, then he slowly closes the door and reaches up to switch on the light. 'Sorry about that, awkward customer,' he explains, getting to his feet just as knocking begins on the front door.

Gary tries again. 'I ...'

'It's ok, I'm pretty sure why you've come. You want to leave us and do an art course. When did you want to start?'

'Er, Monday. I'm sorry. Am I meant to serve notice?'

'No, don't worry about that, we'll manage. We'll miss you of course. I tell you what, why don't you come and work for us in the holidays?'

'I'd like that.'

Room A10 at 9.30 the following Monday contains an assortment of types. There's one woman with sort of oriental clothes, all gold and inky colours; another in her fifties with fair hair shooting out in all directions. She looks as if she's peeping out of a haystack. There's a man with strange, angular features, long, greying hair tied at the back, a shirt that smells of wood smoke, shorts and sandals. Gary feels abnormally normal in his best shirt and trousers. And they all seem to have big, maroon-coloured folders, tied with black cord in a bow in the middle.

There's something familiar about the teacher. Gary stares long and hard at him. He must be in his fifties, balding, with chiselled features and brown paper skin. He's obviously been abroad a long time.

'I'm afraid I don't know any of you,' he says. 'I haven't been here for twenty-one years.'

'Same age as me,' thinks Gary, before noticing that now he is being closely studied.

Nick Price likes the look of this student. Intuition tells him that he has promise. And it's obvious that he does physical work. That's interesting. 'Have you got your portfolio?' he asks Gary.

'Wassat?'

Everyone laughs.

'A folder with your drawings. One of these. He points to Mrs Haystack's portfolio.'

'Oh no, but I've got some drawings. They're at home, like. I'm only down Station Road. I can go and gerr 'em. I'll be back in a shit.'

Everyone laughs again and Gary runs off. In a few minutes, he's back holding a large roll of papers under his arm. He dumps it unceremoniously on the table and it unfolds itself. They crowd round. There are drawings and sketches in biro, marker pen, children's poster paints, pencil; almost every medium. The other students gasp in wonder. The still-life subjects have been grasped in just a few lines and the scenes have a sort of naive perspective, which is striking.

'These are brilliant,' says Nick, chewing at a piece of gum, sitting on the edge of the table, his face all admiration. 'Sorry, I didn't catch your name.'

'Gary Lewis.'

Nick stops chewing. He looks flushed. 'Where did you say you live?'

'Station Road. Twenty-two Station Road.'

'What's your mother's name?'

'Sheila.'

'Well, well, well.' Nick sighs a long, loaded sigh, before he straightens out, as if he's shaking something off. 'I suppose I'd better explain the syllabus to you all then,' he says wanly.

Jim and Mike are standing outside the completed bakehouse. Jim has more or less left Mike to supervise this job. This is a rare and probably final visit, to collect a cheque. Mike has limewashed the external walls a brilliant white. The outer frames of the windows and the front door are in Etruscan red and the opening lights in white. The rest of the village is somewhat put to shame by this little gleaming building. Maybe this is the start of a Porthwen revival.

'I've only just heard about your unusual intruder,' says Jim.

'Yes, I suppose we were the intruder really. But I'm told she's moved on. I was sorry to have missed all the drama.'

A middle-aged couple emerge from the front door of the building and walk down the road. They wave briefly to Mike, who waves back.

'Your first booking?' asks Jim.

'Yes. They love the place. The boys have done a smashing job, Jim. Maybe you should go into building restoration.'

'Hah!'

'Only joking,' laughs Mike, 'I know you prefer to build a bungalow, Jim.'

Acknowledgements

I should like to thank those who have read all or some of the stories in draft form and given their valued feedback.

About the author

Martin Davies qualified in architecture at Nottingham University and has practised in the Cardigan area for much of his life. He designed many bungalows during the 1980s, but then began to specialise in building restoration and spent years working for the National Trust at Llanerchaeron and elsewhere.

He has produced two other publications: 'Save the last of the magic', a booklet which encourages the preservation of our local vernacular architecture; and 'Ancient Causeways Uncovered', which provides evidence for an undiscovered Roman route across the Preselis and up the Ceredigion coast.